THE MOUNTAIN'S SECRET

Mary Fulk Larson

THE MOUNTAIN'S SECRET
By Mary Fulk Larson
Volume 2 of the Custer's Mill Mystery series
Copyright 2017
by LarsonHess, LLC
Broadway, Virginia 22815

All rights reserved. No part of this book may be reproduced or transmitted in any form or by any means, electronic or mechanical, including photocopying, recording, or by any information storage and retrieval system without written permission from the publisher, except for the inclusion of brief quotations in a review.

The Mountain's Secret is a work of fiction. Names, characters, places, and organizations and events portrayed in this novel are either products of the author's imagination or are used fictitiously.

Cover Design and Photography by Kevin Finnegan
Book Design by Merrill Miller
Map Art by Debra Wilson

Printed in the United States
First Edition
Library of Congress Control Number: 2017954739
ISBN 9780692926833

Visit Custer's Mill Mysteries on Facebook
or at www.custersmillmysteries.com

Also by Mary Fulk Larson:
Murder on Rosemary Street (Volume 1 in the series)

Prologue

Friday, October 12, 2012

It was an hour past midnight. The cave was pitch dark, and the constant plop of water droplets made musical tinkling sounds on the hard floor. The slippery, sloping walls evoked a sense of claustrophobia in the three men who occupied its space this particular night. The place was a haven for bats and mold, and musty dampness crept into every pore.

"Dream on. You don't deserve twenty-five percent. Not if I take all the risks." The threat in the man's gruff voice expanded and echoed across the cave. He shone his flashlight full into the eyes of the other man, making him blink and throw up his hand against the unwelcomed brightness.

"Then you'll never see the goods I was going to put into your pot," replied his companion in a plaintive tone. "And that's that. I'll find somebody who appreciates what they're worth. You don't have the brains to see it." With a sudden movement, he shoved the man's flashlight downward and stepped back into the shadow.

"You're in no position to call the shots, you inbred idiot."

"You think *I'm* an idiot? Why, you're a brainless, cold-blooded bully, you a son of a ...." His voice tapered off, as he thought better about using the epithet on the angry man. "Anyhow, I've had my fill of your kind." He fastened his flashlight to his belt, held up his fists and braced himself for the blows he knew would come.

The struggle was visible occasionally as the flashlight's beam jerked and danced across the walls and low ceiling of the hideout as the two men fought. A stack of boxes toppled as the fighters grunted and cursed. A pile of tin cans pitched forward on the floor's uneven surface. In the intermittent darkness, each person landed a sporadic punch.

A dull thud of skull smacking against stone brought momentary silence. The victorious contender stepped up to the prone man and gave his leg a fierce kick.

"Get up, you idiot."

An observer, who had stood watch by the cave's door, flashed his light on a pool of blood that inched across the floor where the man lay at an odd angle against an exposed boulder.

"What have you done?" His voice shook.

"Check his pulse, quick."

The observer knelt by the inert body, placed his fingers on the man's neck and shook his head. "He's dead. Look what you've done. Now what do we do?"

"Shut up, you baby. First, we get rid of his body someplace where nobody will find him for a long time. Then we come back here and look for the loot he's hidden from us. Twenty-five percent...and now we get it all. Come on. Help me drag his body out of here. Get him in the truck, fast."

The night was moonless and a rain-laden wind gusted from the southwest, bending tree branches and stirring the musky scent of the forest. It was just past three a.m. The devil's hour. Bad luck for the man whose body had just rolled down the embankment and splashed into the river.

Rain pelted the surface of the water, and the body, weighed down by two large rocks tied to its torso, settled into the soft silt at the bottom of the river with a quiet gurgle.

The two figures peered over the bank. Satisfied with their work, they crept back through the wind-lashed trees. They took care to brush out their tracks with a pine branch.

Friday

October 12

The Brubaker mansion had overlooked the town of Custer's Mill since 1834. But the house lay dormant now. If ghosts of the past graced the halls and rooms, they would be about their own business.

It had been four months since Bertha Brubaker had died. She was the final matriarch in a long line of Custer's Mill Brubakers. Her great-great-grandfather made the family fortune as a merchant, sailing sea routes to faraway places. It was his vision and money that developed this Shenandoah Valley town.

The house stood on the hill like a sentinel on watch. The elegant three-story Victorian mansion was flanked by a row of columns. The porch, which ran the length of the front of the house, echoed an era gone by. One could imagine ladies in their long dresses carrying parasols as they walked down the sloped lawn toward the rose gardens.

"Can you believe our luck?" said Jane Allman as she stood in the center of the large parlor in awe of her surroundings. "Imagine what this place must have looked like back in its heyday." The retired high school science teacher pushed her short, grey hair back from her face and surveyed the room.

"No, I can't." Marguerite White came to stand near her friend, handkerchief in hand, as she dabbed a stray tear or two. Marguerite did not usually show emotion. Her years in the CIA had trained her to keep an impassive face under most circumstances. But this was different. The recent loss of their friend, Bertha Brubaker, was still fresh and tender. It was right that her memory still brought tears.

"Does anyone say 'heyday' anymore?" said Nanette Steele. "I know what you mean though. This place is way too fancy for me. Give me the barnyard any day." Nanette, resident farmer and quintessential cliché manufacturer, pushed the toe of her ragged work boot against a shiny mahogany table leg.

Although their paths had taken them in diverse directions, the ladies had been friends for many years. And now, the death of the matriarch of Custer's Mill had brought them together for a new adventure. They stood together now, unable to grasp the enormity of Bertha's bequest.

Before lawyer Paul Stuart had read them Bertha's will, not one of them had suspected that Bertha would leave the Brubaker mansion to them. Of course, Bertha had been their friend for decades, but her nephew Billy was the last heir. And even though Bertha had been disappointed with the choices Billy had made throughout most of his life, he still had the legal right to his aunt's worldly goods. Or so they all thought. But here they were, inside the vast walls of the mansion, not as guests, but as co-owners.

"I sure hope Billy has made peace with this whole transaction," said Jane.

"You mean with the fact that we inherited the mansion and he didn't?" Nanette was never one to mince words.

Billy's childhood had been a troubled one. He'd been bullied and intimidated by his classmates and never seemed to fit in with any particular group. In high school, he became involved with several troublemakers, and that association continued into adulthood. Former Custer's Mill Police Chief Pete Anderson had Billy under his thumb. Anderson had blackmailed Billy for years for a part he'd played in a fatal house fire.

Now, Pete was in jail, and Billy was forced to step down from his position of town manager. Shep Crawford, the third member of the group, was on the run.

"I think Billy has learned his lesson," said Marguerite. "Maybe not entirely, but I think he knows he'll never own this place. And now, on to more immediate matters. What will we do with our newfound fortune?"

"Sure is dark in here," said Jane as she pushed back the heavy red brocade curtains that covered all the windows. "There. Much better. Amazing how a bit of sunshine can cheer a place."

"'Cheer' isn't the word I'd use," said Nanette. "This room seems pretty creepy to me. I can't get past the sight of Bertha draped across that velvet settee. Crazy how we all thought she had died of a heart attack, then found out she was poisoned."

"Alright, dears, we need to decide how to best use this gift of Bertha's," said Marguerite. "We each have our own lives and homes. What will we do with a huge place like this?"

"I think we should look at it from Bertha's perspective. Why did she leave it to us?" Jane looked at her two friends. "This home was so important to Bertha and her family. She would expect us to do something creative with it. Maybe a museum?"

"Nice idea, but not quite right." Nanette leaned back in her chair and the wooden frame creaked. "Remember all the good times we had here with Bertha? You know, our gossip sessions, committee meetings, and tea parties."

Marguerite snapped her fingers. "That's it. A tea shop. We need to create a tea shop in memory of Bertha and her hospitality. Just look around you. There are cupboards filled with china tea sets, a pantry full of teas, and plenty of linen tablecloths and napkins. I'll bet if we look around we can find tea strainers, cream pitchers, and sugar bowls."

Jane nodded. "That would no doubt be a place all of Custer's Mill could enjoy. But how would we ever open a business? Three women with no retail or food service experience? Do you think we could manage it?"

Nanette stood up. "I think that's a marvelous idea, Marguerite. A tea shop. I'll bet half of the town would come just to see inside the mansion."

"There are plenty of people who can help. We can hire experts when we need them," Marguerite said. "We knew Bertha better than anyone else in Custer's Mill. I think we could create a tea shop she would be proud of."

Jane looked around the room. "You know, I can almost see it already. And you know what else? I can almost feel Bertha's approval."

"What's all this, Kit Kat?" Custer's Mill police chief Jake Preston took in the collection of objects lined up in a neat row on the kitchen table.

"The stuff I need to take to Nanette's farm. I have a blanket, a flashlight, some peanut butter sandwiches and six bottles of water."

Jake chuckled. "So how long do you think it takes to pick a couple of pumpkins, and why so many bottles of water?"

"We'll need water to drink with the sandwiches, of course," said Kate. "We each get two bottles: two for you, two for Emma, and two for me. You can get thirsty out in those fields, Daddy. Nanette always tells me to be sure to stay hydrated when I'm on the farm."

Jake thought of Emma Kramer, her long, dark brown hair, and that little curl that always seemed to escape. He wasn't going to admit it to Kate, but he found it easy to be around Emma. She defied the stereotype of a librarian—old, stern and formal. She was pretty. And young, only twenty-seven years old. Plus, he noticed more than once that she looked great in jeans and those jeans skirts she liked to wear. But Emma could be stubborn, and sharp-tongued, especially when her childhood friend, Serafina, got under her skin.

"You didn't tell me how long you think this pumpkin-picking party is going to take us." Jake turned his attention back to his daughter. "We're supposed to meet Emma at the library around five o'clock. I didn't think we'd be in the patch more than an hour. After all, we're just gathering pumpkins, not picking out a new car."

Kate tilted her head, and Jake was struck for the hundredth time how much her gestures reminded him of Mirabelle.

"Does it matter if it takes longer? You always say how you work all the time and never get to relax. And Emma says the same thing." Kate gave her father a sidelong glance and began to hop around the room. "I've got a ton of energy to get out. Besides...," she said, offering him the clincher, "Nanette says the pumpkin patch is loaded this year."

"Uh huh," Jake nodded. "And what else do you have up your sleeve?"

"Well, I also thought we could sit in the pumpkin patch and watch the sunset. Or something. Just you, me, and Emma. And maybe Nanette."

"I see. Watch the sunset or something...do you think we might give Emma the wrong impression? After all, watching the sun set in a pumpkin patch while eating peanut butter sandwiches sounds pretty romantic to me." Jake stooped to replace a hair clip that dangled from the side of his daughter's hair.

"Not the wrong idea, Daddy."

So he was 'Daddy' again. Kate had started calling him "Dad," in recent weeks, and he relished the return to the familiar 'Daddy'.

"The right idea," Kate continued. "You know Emma's a really cool lady. And sometimes when she's with us, I pretend we're a family. You know. Three of us instead of two."

"Whoa there, Miss Cupid." Jake frowned. "You know Emma and I are just friends. Good friends, of course, but just friends."

Kate rolled her eyes. "Daddy. I'm almost eight. I notice things. You smile a lot when you're around her. She makes you happy."

"Oh, Kit Kat, don't make too much of my friendship with Emma. I've had enough change in my life for a while. I like our little family of two, for now." Jake pulled his daughter toward him and gave her a hug. "Now, let's get this picnic all packed up. Grab that box of cookies on the counter for dessert, and and see if you can find the picnic basket."

Jake watched as his daughter skipped to the pantry to retrieve the basket for their feast. His heart ached for Kate, growing up without her mother. Mirabelle's death had left them both with a deep void in their lives. Kate was too young to understand how complicated relationships were between adults, especially between a man and a woman. How could he explain to an almost-eight-year-old that he wasn't willing to put his heart out there again?

When he thought Emma had perished in the fire at the library, Jake had felt helpless and alone. He couldn't face the pain of losing someone again. It was better not to let the relationship go beyond the friendship they had. It was best for everyone.

"Look over there, Emma. Can you see them? The pumpkins… the field's full of them, just like Nanette said." Kate bounced up and down in the back seat causing the picnic basket to tumble to the floor.

"Kate, what have I told you about waiting until I stop the car to unbuckle your seatbelt?" said Jake. "And what just hit the floor?"

"It's okay. Just the basket. Nothing spilled."

"Look! There's a million of them!"

"Wow, I see them," said Emma. "Nanette told me the pumpkin crop was good this year, but I had no idea there would be this many. There are pumpkins everywhere."

Jake steered the car into a makeshift parking space. The field was full of people and there were several wagons piled with pumpkins of all sizes and shapes. Nanette waved from the middle of the patch where she helped a toddler carry a huge pumpkin. The little boy's dad had his arms full, and several children danced around him, as each tried to add another pumpkin to his load.

"Hurry, Daddy, I want to go see Nanette. Can you and Emma carry our picnic basket and set the picnic up over there?" Kate pointed to a little hillside at the edge of field. It was shaded by a grove of trees and offered a bird's eye view of Nanette's entire farm.

"You didn't tell me you planned a picnic. What fun," said Emma. "If I had known, I could have brought sandwiches."

"Oh, Kate took care of it all. She made peanut butter sandwiches. We have cold water to drink and cookies for dessert."

Kate beamed.

"You worked so hard, Kit Kat," said Jake. "I thought you might want to set it all up for us."

"I figured you grown-ups could take over since I did the hard part." Kate crossed her arms and tapped her foot. "You know we talked about this."

Jake laughed, and Emma looked confused.

"See, Daddy, I told you that you were happy when you were around Emma."

"What's all this about?" asked Emma.

"Nothing," Jake focused his attention on a huge cricket that had started to crawl up the basket. "Kate just has a big imagination and a lot of romantic ideas."

"Oh?" Now Emma focused on the cricket as well, watching as its stick-like legs latched onto the wicker basket.

Kate scowled. "I do have an imagination, Daddy, but I don't have to use it when I see you around Emma. She makes you laugh. You know that."

"We're buddies, Kate. Just that. You're happy when you're around your friends, right? Emma is my friend, and she makes me happy." He glanced at Emma for support, but her eyes were still on the black insect.

Jake lifted the basket out of the car's trunk and handed Emma the blanket. "Why don't you run along and find Nanette, Kate? We'll set these things down and meet you in a few minutes. Sound good?"

Kate gave an exaggerated sigh, but took off in the direction of her friend.

"If you can manage the blanket, Emma, I'll take the basket."

Jake didn't notice the hurt in Emma's eyes as she followed him over to the hillside.

Saturday

October 13

Saturday morning dawned bright and clear. A warm southern breeze tried to overcome a chilly northwest wind, and scattered high clouds raced in both directions. The northwest wind would prevail. It would be much colder by nightfall.

Only the most intrepid fishermen were out at dawn, in search of a few quiet pools where they could cast their lines. Nine-year-old Noah Lambert was one such sportsman. He'd been tempted to skip school yesterday. His buddy Nate's dad told him that they'd just unloaded trout in the upper branch of the river. It was rare to have a fresh trout stock this late in the year. Noah longed to fill his stringer one more time before cold weather set in.

But he waited until today. Skipping school, however much he was tempted, was wrong. And Noah's mom and dad made sure that he had a clear picture of what was right and what was wrong. Not to mention his Grandpa Hiram. He had a whole list of Bible verses he quoted about darkness and light, good and evil.

Today was Saturday, and Noah could cast his line with a clear conscience. If he was lucky, there would be some fish left. Recently his fishing hole had become more popular than he wanted. Seemed like the whole town was more popular. His parents said the new road made the town famous and now more people were visiting. There were a lot of folks who made a detour through Custer's Mill just to see some of the historic spots they'd read about in the papers. Too many people for Noah.

He sighed and patted his yellow lab, Lightning, on the top of his damp head. Lightning gave an appreciative snort and settled himself in the wet foliage at the top of the bank. He watched as Noah prepared the tackle for his first catch.

Noah liked to fish in several areas back in this part of the forest. Today, he decided on a deeper spot along a protected bank where the current might not be as fast. A gust of wind allowed a ray of sun to shine through the trees and a glint at the water's edge caught his attention. He set his pole aside and jumped down the bank.

Tall weeds and bits of rotting sticks and logs lay along the waterside. Noah balanced himself and reached past them into the shallow water. It was a coin! He pulled it from its resting place between two stones and wiped it dry on his jeans.

"This is a lucky charm, boy." Noah turned the coin over and over and showed it to Lightning, who had followed him to the water. "Maybe it's real silver. Bet I'll get a big catch today." He ruffled the dog's fur and tucked the treasure deep into his pocket, humming under his breath.

The coin was strange, not like any he'd ever seen. Maybe it was from Civil War times. Or who knows? Maybe even from the Revolutionary War. Might be worth a lot of money.

Noah continued to prepare his line and made a cast into the center of the calmer water. He settled back onto the tarp to wait for a bite. It gave him time to soak in the forest sounds and smells. When he grew up, he would be a forest ranger and live in the woods all the time.

It was only a minute before Noah felt a pull on his line. He tugged at the pole as he gave the line a chance to play out. This was a big one. He began to reel it in and saw movement at the water line.

Then he gasped. "Lightning, what *is* that?" Lightning stood and barked. He sniffed the air as he responded to the alarm in Noah's voice.

A hand. His line was hooked to a plaid red shirt that had someone's arm in it. Noah dropped the fishing pole and it slid down the bank until it caught in the branch of a large dead tree. He grabbed his pack and ran down the wooded path as he pulled his cell phone from his jacket pocket to call 911. Like his parents taught him to do in emergencies. This was an emergency.

"Yes, this is Noah Lambert, and I...I just f-found a dead body in the river. I was fishing and I saw a hand and...and...Yes, ma'am." He paused and took a deep breath, as instructed by the dispatcher. Then he began to explain where he was and agreed to wait near the county road for a police car to arrive. His hands shook as he ended the call. He buried his face in Lightning's fur, as he held back sobs. "Oh, Lightning..."

Finally, he gathered his courage, and walked down the rocky path toward the road. He'd show the police the way to the horrible thing he'd discovered.

Chief Jake Preston mentally checked off the items on his to-do list. Small town policemen didn't get days off, they got stolen moments between minor crises.

He'd just dropped Kate off at the church for Saturday Morning Kids Club, and now he had to get serious about his tasks. He made imaginary tic marks in his mind: Take their cat Delphinium to the vet for her annual visit; get the second *Lemony Snickett* book for Kate at the library; take his blue suit to the dry cleaners. He also had to stop by lawyer Paul Stewart's office.

The past several months had been a whirlwind of life-changing events. The incident that had stayed on his mind the most was the unexpected legacy that his young daughter inherited. Most people don't suddenly have that kind of money dumped on their doorstep. He'd never seen anything like it. But Kate inherited more than money. A substantial amount of property had also been a part of old Bertha Brubaker's bequest.

Of course Kate had no idea what an extraordinary inheritance had come her way. Or at least he hoped not. But he knew the speed at which news travels in small towns. He was sure that by year's end, he would need to explain to his daughter that she was a wealthy young lady. Or would be when she turned twenty-one.

But now was not the time to muse. He'd save these thoughts for nights when he couldn't sleep. Like most nights. No amount of warm milk or Sleepytime tea could keep his mind from its incessant activity.

He was so lost in thought that he almost passed by the blue truck along the side of the road. He saw the white plastic bag stuck in its window just in time to slam on the brakes. A small, elderly man stood beside the upraised hood.

"Need some help there, sir?" Jake asked as he approached the truck.

The man's bright blue eyes sparkled in a sea of wrinkles. "Well, much obliged, Mr. Policeman. Ol' Betsy decided not to start again. I stopped here to look at a plant I thought might be ginseng." He took off his cap and ran his fingers through his hair. "But it was just a weed. A patch of Virginia Creeper." He extended his gnarled hand to Jake. "Petey Blue here."

Jake shook the man's hand. Petey Blue smiled and showed a row of crooked teeth. "You new in these parts, Officer? I don't recollect seeing you here before. But then, I haven't been in town for a long while. I'm here to stay with my aunt for a season."

Petey Blue scratched his forehead. "You know Bessie Crawford? Her grand-boy, Shep, used to take care of her. But you probably know, he up and took off. Some kind of tangled mess with the law."

Before Jake could formulate an answer, the passenger door of the truck opened and a gangly, skinny man gave Jake a solemn look.

"Marv don't say much. I almost always talk for both of us." Petey Blue patted his friend on the shoulder. "Marv's the brains and I'm the mouth." He snickered at his own joke and looked at Jake. "So you're a cop, huh?"

"Yes sir." Jake had moved to look under the hood of the truck. The battery terminals were corroded with half an inch of gunk. No wonder the engine wouldn't turn over. Jake was surprised it had gotten the men this far.

"We live on the mountain over there." Petey Blue made a vague gesture toward the west. "Top of Feedstone. Know where that is? Over on the West Virginia side."

"I've seen it on a topographical map. They have one on the wall just inside the Spare Change Diner. Pretty interesting land formations around here."

"Topo maps don't tell it all. It's a lot rougher country than them green lines let on. We come down every month or so to get supplies. Most times we go into West Virginia, though. We also do a little spying on our own. Right Marv?"

Marv's mouth moved into a tight smile.

"Spying?" Jake looked at Petey Blue. "What kind of spying?

"We've done a little investigating in our time, ain't we Marv?" He didn't wait for an answer. "Mostly stuff from a ways back. You know, skeletons in the closet, sins of the fathers."

Jake started. Where had he heard that expression before, 'sins of the fathers'? He narrowed his eyes and looked at Petey Blue. "It's been my experience that most people like to let sleeping dogs lie. You know, keep the past in the past. Do you get a lot of call for your kind of work?"

"More than you might think, Officer. Just last week Marv and me ran all over the mountain doing our best to identify an old picture. Marge Clayborne said it was her daddy, but her cousin Peggy said it was the postmaster. Turns out they were both right." He winked at Jake.

Jake returned the wink. "Like I said, sometimes it's just best to let bygones be bygones. By the way, looks like you have a bit of a buildup on your battery. Let me scrape some of the stuff off and then I'll hook up the jumper cables and rev the engine again. But we'll have to get you into town to get a new battery. This one won't get you up Jenkins Hollow Road, if you're heading to Mrs. Crawford's, that is."

Petey Blue ruffled his thin, graying hair. "Mighty nice of you, Officer. Much nicer than that slacker that called himself a policeman. You know, the one that was in office before you? I don't think anybody was sorry to see him get locked away."

Petey Blue spat into a clump of chicory by the side of the road. "No sir. Didn't much care for that Anderson man. He could look you straight in the eye while he stabbed you in the back. He had ol' Shep at his beck and call. I mean when you can get somebody to murder for you, you got 'em wrapped around your finger."

Jake continued to clean the battery nodes without comment. Had it been only three months since he'd put former Custer's Mill Police Chief Pete Anderson behind bars? He didn't like to think about how they almost lost Emma to Pete's murderous intentions.

"Yessiree, I know old Shep had some problems, but he never would have killed Miss Brubaker if he wasn't pressured mighty hard from somebody who held something over him, big time."

Jake nodded, but continued to focus on scraping the battery without comment.

Not one to let silence build, Petey Blue continued. "Ol' Marv here used to court the late Miss Bertha. Remember that, Marv? You used to make half a dozen trips a week up and down that mountain."

Marv blushed a brilliant red. Petey Blue, oblivious to his friend's discomfort continued. "Yeah, you and Bertha were quite an item even though she was a good bit older than you. We all thought you'd get hitched someday." He shook his head. "Guess you just couldn't live up to daddy's expectations, though. You'd think old Brubaker would have recognized quality, even if it was dressed in patched overalls and work boots."

Jake tried to hide his surprise. Marv and Miss Bertha? Hardly a likely pair.

"But in the end, though, I'm glad it didn't work out. "Can't trust rich people. That's what I always tell Marv. Watch out for them rich ones. Even our Lord himself said it was easier for a camel to go through the eye of a needle than for a rich man to enter the kingdom."

When he heard the scripture verse roll off Petey Blue's tongue, Jake wondered if the older man knew the Brubaker estate gardener, Hiram Steinbacher. Those two would be quite a pair.

Jake wiped his hands on his handkerchief and hooked up the jumper cables. "I think that does it. I'll start my cruiser and get that engine purring again. I'll follow you into town to make sure your truck doesn't stop."

The mountain man looked up and down the highway. He leaned in closer and whispered, "We alone?"

"Far as I know. You, me and Marv. What's up?"

"I wasn't sure I should bring this up since you're new and we don't know you and all, but I think you're a man to be trusted. What do you think, Marv?"

Marv nodded, and Petey Blue hunched even closer. Jake wanted to step back from the small man and the strong scent of garlic on his breath, but he steeled himself and stood still.

"Me and Marv here have found a treasure. A treasure that might be worth a lot of money." Jake raised an eyebrow.

"You know back in the early 1900s when the American chestnut blight happened?"

"I think I heard about a chestnut blight. Some kind of fungus that gets into the trees, isn't it?"

"All but destroyed the entire lot of trees. Not just here in the Shenandoah Valley, but all over the east coast. About four billion trees died. Only a couple of places in the country where someone has found trees that didn't get the blight, outside of the main area where they usually grew.

"Supposedly, only a couple, that is." The man turned and gave Marv a secretive glance.

Jake shifted to one foot. He hoped Petey Blue would get to the moral of the story soon. His head had started to throb. He suspected it came from holding his nose just at the right angle to escape the brunt of the rush of garlic on the man's breath.

The mountain man moved in closer. "'Til now, everybody thought there weren't any more American chestnuts left in these mountains. But me and Marv here know that's not true. Show him, Marv."

Marv reached into his pocket. He drew out a wrinkled print of a stand of tall, stately trees. "Look here." He thrust the picture in front of Jake. "What do you see?"

Jake held the picture back from his face and inspected it. "Looks like some trees in the woods."

"Not just any trees, man. These here are a hundred percent, American chestnut trees. Big ones, too. Yessiree, we found the trees everybody's been looking for in these mountains." Petey Blue stepped back and grinned like a Cheshire cat. "We done found us a miracle."

"That's quite an accomplishment, boys. Where'd they come from?"

Petey Blue shrugged. "We need to make sure these trees stay healthy and don't show any sign of that blight. Might be they're extra healthy and could help repopulate the forests. If we tell the press, we'd have a million people loose in the woods, scaring the deer and makin' a mess. No, we'll just sit tight on this find for, say, the next fifty or so years."

Jake looked at the two men. They were at least seventy now. Their chances of sitting on this knowledge for more than ten or so more years were pretty slim.

"I know what you think, officer. You think these geezers are riding their last rodeo, now. Why are they worried about the next fifty years?"

Jake smiled. "That thought did cross my mind, I'll admit."

"We want you to help us find some young'un who we can trust with our secret. Some bright, smart young feller who will keep watch over this grove of trees long after we're gone to our reward." Marv took off his hat and laid it across his chest as if he already stood by Petey Blue's grave.

"Well, I don't know…"

"No, not now. I know you're new here," said Petey. "But in time when you get to know the people better, I want you to tell us the name of somebody we can talk to. Somebody to continue our charge. You'll know when the right one comes along."

Petey Blue touched Jake's shoulder as if to commission him for the task ahead. In the brief silence, Jake smiled to himself. There were many places more exciting than Custer's Mill. But he doubted that any other town on the face of God's green earth had such a cast of peculiar characters.

Petey Blue's face broke into a wide grin. "Now, hook us up, sir. We're ready to roll."

Just as the engine turned over in the cruiser, Jake felt his pager buzz.

"Ten-fifty-four down at the North Fork near Ed's Gas Station. All units report to the scene."

Ten-fifty-four? Jake grabbed his cell phone. A ten-fifty-four was a dead body.

"Who in Sam Hill has trashed these shelves? Don't they teach the alphabet in schools anymore these days?" Volunteer Nanette Steele pushed the overloaded book cart down the fiction aisle, still muttering under her breath. "I've never seen such a jumbled mess in all my seventy years. Guess kids have better ways to spend their time than put library books away."

"Well in all of *my* years, I've learned one thing—a volunteer's work is never done." Marguerite grabbed a book just as it was about to tip off the cart. "By the way, who taught you to load a book cart?"

Nanette scowled.

Marguerite shelved her two books and reached for more from the crammed cart. "At least we had a good reason not to be here. It's not every day you inherit a mansion."

"I hope she didn't expect all three of us to live in it." Jane Allman walked by with a load of DVDs. "I can see that now. Nanette's goats would eat the roses, Marguerite's *avant garde* furniture would look odd in the parlor, and my geology reference books would clash with the antique walnut bookcases."

"Wonder why she didn't leave anything to our Emma?" said Marguerite.

"Well, she didn't know that Emma would be the one to solve her murder, now did she? How many librarian sleuths do you know?" said Nanette. "Heck, she didn't even have a clue that our vile police chief and his wretched sidekick would eliminate one of the two Custer's Mill Brubakers left on earth. I'd say that Bertha Brubaker was one unwary victim."

"How many wary victims do you know?" Marguerite winked.

"You know what I mean, Ms. Word Nerd." Nanette poked her friend with her elbow.

"At least our wicked ex-police chief now has a long-term bunk reserved for him at the federal prison," said Marguerite. "And I'm glad Jake Preston is our new police chief."

"Yeah," agreed Nanette. "Now if they could just find that no good rascal, Shep Crawford. But that's not our worry. Right now, I'd be happy just to unload this cart."

"Thank heavens for miracles," said Emma as she strode across the room to greet the women. "I thought I would never recover from this mess. She gestured at the piles of books on the counter. I was afraid you three had flown the coop."

Marguerite sighed. "I know we've left you in the lurch, Emma, but…well, we've been a bit preoccupied lately. You see…"

"Yes…?" Emma leaned forward, eager to hear more.

But before any of them could say another word, the front door of the library opened and two rather scruffy old men stood in the foyer. Both men blinked in the bright, fluorescent light and looked around in wonder as though they'd just stepped onto an alien planet.

"Wow. Just look at what modern technology has done, Marv. Why, there's a whole row of computers."

Nanette rolled her eyes.

"Oh, 'scuse me, ladies. I'm being a bit on the rude side. I'm hopin' you can forgive me, though. I was taken aback with all of this modern grandeur."

"Modern?" Nanette growled. "This place was built before the Civil War."

"You know what I mean. All of these portals to the World Wide Web."

A gleam of recognition settled over Nanette's face. "Why, Petey Blue Silas Crawford, what business do you have off Feedstone Mountain? I almost didn't recognize you, you've been gone so long."

Petey Blue stepped back. "Pardon me for worryin', but nobody ever uses all four of my names unless I'm in a heap of trouble."

"You silly old fool." Nanette clapped him on the back. "Good to see you."

Emma and Marguerite looked from Petey Blue to Nanette, waiting for an introduction.

"Sorry. These two old fogies are my buddies from way back. Jane and I are well acquainted with them, but let me introduce them to you two ladies. Emma, Marguerite, meet Petey Blue Crawford and Marv Holloway. We went to school together, and have tramped a few mountains in our day." Nanette paused, lost in thought about an earlier, happier time.

Jane gave the men a warm handshake. "Gentlemen. Delighted to see you both again."

"Pleased to see you Miss Jane, and to make your acquaintance, ladies." Petey Blue doffed an imaginary hat and Marv nodded.

"Remember when Marv got lost back at Slate Lick?" Nanette was determined to revisit the past.

Marv shuffled his feet and looked uncomfortable.

"Got lost, my foot. He was sneaking away to pay a call on Miss Bertha Brubaker," said Petey.

All four ladies shifted their attention to the man's companion.

"Miss Brubaker?" said Emma.

"Aw, Marv looks uneasy. We'll discuss his romantic life at another time in another place. Right now, we have some library business." He cleared his throat. "Some mighty important library business."

"Oh yeah? So what kind of 'library business' brings you two hoboes into town?" Nanette looked suspicious.

"Truck broke down on Highway 11. Your kind police chief offered us his services. But he got an emergency alert on his pager. So he called the tow truck to drop us off here. We're just waiting for the folks over at Ed's to check our battery or do whatever they have to, to get us back on the road."

"So you didn't come to the library on purpose." Nanette said. "Just a stopover while you wait for your truck? That makes a lot more sense."

"Wait. You said Chief Preston had an emergency call?" Emma interrupted the friendly banter. "Any idea what happened? I didn't hear rescue sirens.

"No, the good lawman didn't choose to fill us in on the details. He just called Ed's Towing Service for us, and here we are. If you don't mind to show us how to run those computers over there, we could do some research while we're here." Petey Blue gave Nanette a lopsided smile and winked at Marv.

"Yep, us country hicks have joined the modern world and learned a bit about the information highway," he continued. "This afternoon, we're headin' Bessie's way, and I know she's gonna send us into the woods to gather plants, now the rain's stopped. I'd just as soon know what we're looking for."

Jane cleared her throat. "That will be fine, gentlemen. Do either of you have a library card?"

Marv looked at Petey Blue and shook his head. "Now, don't feel bad, Marv. We don't often find ourselves in a position to need the services of such a fine establishment."

Petey Blue looked back at Jane and said, "But, I'll be happy to provide you with some identification if you will be so kind as to issue me a library card. And our new domicile will be with my Aunt Bessie for a while. Poor old soul." Petey Blue reached into his back pocket and pulled out a battered wallet.

"Great," said Jane. "Here's the library card application. Just complete it and you're good to go."

"Hey, I need help over here," a young man in overalls and a plaid shirt stood at one of the computer stations. He waved his arms like a drowning man in a storm. "Can anybody help me? This dumb machine froze on me while I was in the middle of this job application. I'm not gonna type in all of this stuff again."

"Okay, okay. Keep your shirt on. I'll be right there," said Nanette. "Think I've got wings on my feet or something?" The young man muttered under his breath and sat back down.

Petey Blue pulled his chair next to the circulation desk and began to write his information on the form. His large handwriting filled the narrow spaces.

On the other side of the desk, Jane and Marguerite had other matters on their minds. "We don't want some fly-by-night charlatan," said Jane, "I've heard that criminals sometimes pose as itinerant painters to make extra money on the run. Besides, those walls are old, and we want to keep the spirit of the place even if we do spruce it up a bit. We need somebody who can respect the character of the house."

"Well, we need more than a painter," said Marguerite. "You can bet we'll have to do some overall maintenance and repairs too—you know check the electrical wires and the plumbing."

Emma pulled a cart over to the computers and leaned on the desk. "Okay, ladies. Out with it. I want to hear what you three have decided to do with the Brubaker mansion."

"Well," said Marguerite in a low voice, "if you really want to know…"

Emma gave her an impatient glance.

Marguerite smiled and continued. "We've decided to turn the Brubaker mansion into a tea shop."

"Whoa. Seriously? Nice! In fact, that's the best news I've heard since Uncle Albert told us the library wouldn't be torn down by a road crew."

Marguerite put her finger to her lips. "It's not like we've told anybody yet, so keep all of this under your hat, if you would. We still have a tremendous number of details to manage."

"I'll bet. I would have no idea where to begin," said Emma.

"You know," said Jane, "Hosting teas in that formal parlor was one of Bertha's favorite rituals, and we thought it would be the perfect way to share the mansion with all the citizens of Custer's Mill."

"Super." Emma surveyed the piles of papers stacked by her desk and the winter reading program flyers she'd just copied. This news was a double-edged sword. How would she ever get all of her work done at the library if her most faithful volunteers were busy serving tea and scones to the citizens of Custer's Mill?

"And we thought we could add some books," said Jane. "We want our venerable local bookseller, Laurence George, to set up a spot to display some historical volumes on the Shenandoah Valley."

"Since the tourists have started to take notice of Custer's Mill, we thought we'd capitalize on the fact that travelers love to read the history of the places they've been," Marguerite added.

"Yes," said Jane, "And I heard they might even open Fort Run Caverns, again. It's supposed to be filled with a lot of Civil War soldiers' names—carvings by soldiers who hid there."

Nanette leaned on her elbows and moved closer to Emma. "People say there are some pretty valuable relics still buried somewhere in that maze of caverns."

Emma shuddered. "Well, given my recent experience with tunnel travel, I don't think I'll be spelunking any time soon, treasure or no treasure."

Nanette nodded. "Yeah, thank goodness for that tunnel, or you wouldn't have escaped the fire at the library. Set by that killer, Pete Anderson. Somebody told me that all those tunnels connect, and Custer's Mill is on top of one big labyrinth of caves."

"Just think, a few months ago, we were worried that the highway department planned to tear down our library to build the new superhighway," Emma said.

"What fun we had as amateur detectives, digging into town history." Marguerite said. "But now, I suppose we'll have to hang up our trench coats and don flowered aprons." She looked almost disappointed.

"Well, ladies, I love your tea shop idea, and I know Bertha would be pleased. But I have to ask. Does this mean you won't be able to help at the library any more?" Emma tried not to sound distressed.

"Now what do you think?" Jane placed her hand on Emma's arm. "Why in heaven's name would we work to save the place and then abandon it? We'll be here, my dear. Don't you worry. In fact, Marguerite and I just discussed how we might find some hired help. Someone to help us take care of the place. We've started writing a classified ad to put into the newspaper."

"Did I hear the word 'help'?" None of the ladies had noticed that Petey Blue had completed his library card form and now stood by the desk. "Me and Marv here are real handy with a hammer and saw."

"What about a paint brush?" said Nanette who had solved the dilemma of the frozen computer and had joined the group gathered in the front of the library. "We want to repaint those rooms right away. Those old walls could use a couple coats of something cheery."

Petey Blue bowed. "Painting is our specialty, my dear ladies. Give us a brush and we'll work miracles. Right, Marv?" Marv nodded.

"When could you start?" asked Marguerite.

"Day before yesterday." Petey Blue looked around to see if anybody thought his joke was funny. Three pairs of eyes stared at him. He cleared his throat. "We could start Monday morning, ma'am."

"Well, if you two are half as good as you think you are, why do you travel around the country like a couple of hoboes?" Nanette looked doubtful.

"We're just between jobs at the moment," said Petey Blue. "Got a couple of projects underway. We have to take care of a few loose ends before we look for more permanent work."

"Well, what do you think, ladies? Maybe we don't need this ad. Have we got ourselves some painters?" Jane glanced at her two friends.

"We know the address all right," said Petey Blue. "Old Marv here hasn't forgot how to get to Miss Bertha's house, have you, Marv? Why, your old feet could take you there even if your eyes were closed."

Marv's elbow shot out and jabbed Petey Blue in the ribs. "Shut up, Petey, that was a long time ago. And she's gone now, anyhow." He looked down again.

The ladies stared at each other in astonishment. Even Petey Blue looked taken aback at this unaccustomed outburst from the normally taciturn man.

Nanette broke the stunned silence. "Okay, I guess I'm game. I'm still not sure this is the smartest action to take. I'm afraid we might be in for more than we bargained for. Stop by here next week, and we'll let you know when we want you to start."

The last patrons had left. The library was quiet and the doors were locked. Emma was tired, but she loved this part of her day. The empty space gave her a sense of satisfaction. All the books and magazines were in neat rows and stacks, the returns box was ready to receive books that were dropped off, and the chairs at the computer tables were straight and even. Her desk was cleared and Monday's work lay in a tidy stack in the silver inbox.

She gathered her lunch bag and tote, and jingled her car keys. "You need five items at the store," she reminded herself. "Eggs, milk, swiss cheese…."

A raspy noise at the back door cut her recitation short. Alert, she stood for a moment, rooted in the doorway of her office. Then in rapid strides, she reached the door and threw it open.

Serafina Wimsey stepped back on the concrete stoop and bowed with a flourish. Her flowing turquoise skirt accentuated her narrow waist, and her long, red-gold hair was pulled back with a mother of pearl clasp. She held a metal nail file in her hand and waved it at Emma, a mischievous smile on her face.

"Serafina. What's the big idea? You can't just pick a lock and come in whenever you feel like it. We're closed and I'm on my way home."

"Chill, Emma. Come on, I just need to send a quick fax to one of my suppliers who never uses computers. Not yet anyway—I hope they'll join the twenty-first century soon." Serafina waved a paper in front of her face. "Only a faxed order will do. No harm in that, right?

"Yes there is harm in that. You broke into the library. We're closed, and you can't use the fax machine. You'll have to come back in the morning. After we're open. Officially open. That means at ten a.m. and not before. *Capiche?* "

"Oh, I love it when you talk Italian, Emma. And, say, whatever happened to that trip to Europe you always used to talk about? You know, Italy, Switzerland, Germany." Serafina looked dreamy. "I've been to all those countries. You should have gone when you had the chance."

She paused. "Now, I just need to fax this one teensy weensy page."

"I said not now, Serafina. You have to come back when we're open." Emma stepped over to the fax machine and stood in front of it, arms stiff at her side like a palace guard. She stared at Serafina with a fixed, blank look.

"Well, doesn't that beat all. Emma, the spinster librarian, keeping her precious machine safe from the evil fax monster." Serafina's laugh was sharp and unpleasant.

"Monster is about right, Serafina. You do resemble a monster to me. You've been one of my worst nightmares for about five years now. Since college. Since the fire that killed Eric. At the party *you* invited him to."

"Now, now, Emma. You know Eric was tired of you. He found me just a lot more… well, lively, maybe? *Dull* is your middle name, my old friend. You never realized your dream of a European adventure. You don't even have a boyfriend now, and you're the librarian. A *librarian*, of all things. In this one-horse town, back home where you were raised. How sad is that?"

Emma recoiled and fought the desire to rush at Serafina. Punch her. Kick her. Do anything to make her feel some pain. Like the pain Emma had felt for years, ever since Eric died. Instead, she took a deep breath, gathered her emotions and held them in check.

"You need to leave. Now. And if I ever find you breaking into the library again, picking locks or cracking windows, I'll report you to the police. Leave." She pointed to the door.

Serafina grinned and curtseyed. "Yes, mum. I'll just leave now. Out the servant's entrance, your majesty. High and mighty, just like old times."

She swung open the door and turned back to Emma with a look of malice. "Thanks, dear friend. I won't forget this great favor." And she was gone.

Emma trembled. She leaned against the back door for a minute to compose herself. At least, she thought, she had kept her anger in check, but Serafina's words had hurt. Emma felt them in the air. They taunted her. *"Eric was tired of you…Dull is you your middle name…never realized your dreams…back home where you were raised."* Angry tears welled in Emma eyes and her chest tightened.

She gathered her tote bag and left the library. Grief washed over her. She'd lost her mother, her boyfriend, and all of those dreams she'd held dear in college. What had happened to the vivacious girl who planned to travel the world and be so happy?

Was she a bitter recluse? A crabby old spinster?

Emma sighed with relief when she saw her aunt Mia's car in the garage. She had driven the few blocks from the library to Mia's house in an anxious fog but just the sight of the familiar Victorian house made her relax. No matter how turbulent her life, her aunt could always help her make sense of any situation.

"Oh my, Emma. What's happened? It's not your father…?" Mia stepped aside and allowed Emma to enter. Mia was the only sister of Emma's father. She had never married, and was beloved by Emma as confidante and mentor.

"No, Dad's okay." Emma collapsed on the sofa, holding back tears. "It's Serafina. Sh-she broke into the library and attacked me."

"She what?" asked Mia. "Did she hit you?

"No, it wasn't like that." Emma reached for a tissue on the side table. "She used that nail file trick of hers to break into the library."

Mia raised an eyebrow. "And?"

"Don't you think that was enough?" Emma regretted her tone

the moment the words left her mouth, but her aunt didn't seem to notice.

"I'm sorry, Aunt Mia. I just feel stressed. I didn't mean to snap at you. But the nerve of Serafina. She thought it was okay to break in the back door of the library since the front door was locked. She needed to fax an order. When I told her the library was closed and that she'd have to come back tomorrow, she got nasty."

"How so?"

Emma took a deep breath. "She told me I was dull and that Eric had grown tired of me. She pretty much said that my life was a failure." Emma balled her fists and willed the unshed tears to stay inside.

Mia moved to sit next to Emma. "You don't believe any of this do you, Emma? Just take a minute to think about it. You have a stable career. You're admired as the librarian in our town. People come to you for information and advice. What has Serafina done? Her free spirit might have been fetching when she was a teenager, but you're both grown women now. Do you think she might be a tad bit jealous of you?"

Emma's eyes widened. "You have to be kidding. Serafina is one of the most self-satisfied people I know."

"Maybe on the outside. But no one knows what a person really feels." Mia looked toward the bay window facing the town of Custer's Mill. "I think you're at a standstill, waiting for the miracle to come, Emma—like the Leonard Cohen song says. You haven't tried to make a better future for yourself. I know you've had a hard time with all that's happened to you over the past few years, but child, you can still make choices for today. And you have so many things Serafina could be jealous of…your job, your house, your family."

"Now don't look so incredulous, Emma. We all have bad days, even free floaters like Serafina. You remember what her mother was like—fickle, alcoholic, and irresponsible. Serafina has never known the stability of a family that cares for her. I know this doesn't make it all better, but sometimes it helps to look at a situation from a different perspective once in a while."

"I have to admit," Emma said, "her words did have some truth to them. I am back home, I haven't traveled like I had wanted to, and many of my friends from school are married with families. I don't even have a boyfriend."

"Well, you have a professional career and that takes a lot of your time. And just because you haven't traveled yet, doesn't mean you won't in the future. As far as a man in your life, I would say you're pretty smitten with our new police chief and he seems to like you."

Emma stared at her aunt. "Are you serious? He hasn't taken his eyes off Serafina since the moment she waltzed into his line of vision. And he told me recently he considered me just a friend."

"Perhaps. Men are often fascinated with glitter and high spirits. But glitz and glamour don't last forever." Her voice trailed off. Both women sat in silence for a few moments.

"At any rate, I think it's time you take responsibility for choices you *can* make. If you're interested in Jake Preston, go for it…if you want to travel, make plans. When you were a little girl, one of your favorite book characters was Harriet the Spy. That carefree and inquisitive spirit you had as a child is still inside of you. You just have to discover it again."

Both women jumped as the doorbell cut through their conversation. Mia went to the door and returned with Albert Nelson, Emma's great uncle on her mother's side. His research had helped save the library from demolition just a few months ago, and now the building was designated as an historical landmark.

"What a sight to behold. Two gorgeous ladies aglow in the autumn sunshine." He bowed and both women dropped mock curtseys.

"What a charmer you are, Uncle Albert." Emma gave him a hug and stepped back to straighten his bow tie. Albert had always been her mother's favorite uncle. Emma loved him too.

"You look rather dapper as well. Where are you headed?"

"Why this gorgeous lady has agreed to accompany me to the new Italian restaurant in Staunton. You know, the one that got the rave reviews in the *Custer's Mill Star*?"

"Wait a minute. I had no idea," said Emma. "Have I missed something here? I've heard rumors that folks have seen the two of you about town together. What's up?"

"Well, child, don't seem so surprised," Uncle Albert replied. "There is still some life left in these old bones, and Mia seems to like my company. She was a great help to me when I did all of that research to declare the library a historical landmark."

"But, Albert, it was *your* work that saved our library." Mia took the professor's arm.

"Still, I thought you would have said something, Aunt Mia."

"We don't expect you to keep track of the lives of all of the citizens of Custer's Mill," said Mia. "You have your own life to lead."

"Funny. We were just talking about that, weren't we?"

"Yes and we can finish the conversation later, or maybe you already know what your next step will be." Aunt Mia smiled. "Remember what I said, Emma. You're not a victim of your circumstances. You have choices."

The yellow police tape vibrated in the breeze. There was no doubt as to the identity of the body discovered by Noah Lambert. It was Shep Crawford.

"To think he was this close," Jake muttered. He kicked a stick that lay in the path. Had Shep hidden in the mountains since summer when Pete Anderson was arrested? And why was he here at the river? This was no accident, but who would want to murder him?

The police had looked for Shep Crawford for over three months after he was implicated in Bertha Brubaker's death. Jake had extracted very little information from Shep's old grandmother, Bessie, as to the whereabouts of her grandson. She'd just stared at him with those raisin-like eyes and shook her head.

"Mrs. Crawford knows where he's been hiding. I'm sure of it." Jake turned to his deputy, Jason Dove. "We'll go to her place in a bit. As far as I know, she's Shep's next of kin. Maybe we can get information from her, now that Shep's dead."

Dove nodded. "Somebody gave him food and basic supplies these past months, but I don't think old Mrs. Crawford would be strong enough to take anything to him herself. Unless he came to her at night or something."

"We have some new visitors to town I'll need to talk to as well. They say they're connected to Bessie Crawford in some way."

Jake walked back to where several investigators canvassed the area around the body. Another officer escorted the county medical examiner to where the corpse lay.

"That crime scene just doesn't make sense, sir." Dove gestured toward the forest behind the river. "I looked around in the woods and found some drag marks. Looks like somebody pulled a pretty bulky object over the leaves. Funny thing is, I don't see any boot or shoe prints. And with all the rain we've had, there should be some."

"Show me what you saw," said Jake. "I haven't tracked much in the forest, so I'll count on you to find details that might reveal hiding places around here. I want to talk with young Noah Lambert soon. He was very brave. Let's head to Jenkins Hollow as soon as we finish here."

"Sure thing, Chief. Now if you'll follow me, I'll show you where it looks like footprints were brushed away."

The late afternoon sun created a thin line of light as it filtered through the tall evergreens in the little hollow just below the top of Jenkins Knob. Although the day was mild for mid-October, Serafina shivered as her bare feet touched the damp leaves of the forest floor.

Several yards ahead of her, Bessie Crawford stopped to scratch at the dirt with the toe of a worn, leather boot. "Bring the shovel here, girl. Burdock root." Serafina bent over the spot of rough earth and saw nothing but a tiny mound of leaves. "Are you sure? Looks like bare ground to me."

Bessie spat a stream of foul-smelling tobacco juice near Serafina's foot and snatched the shovel. "Same spot as belladonna," the old woman muttered. "The purple shade will cool the fire and douse the flame of life. Grab tight the reins of the pale horse and soar above its shadowy rule."

Her effort was rewarded as a fawn-colored tentacle appeared in the dark loam. "Yes." Bessie raised her eyes as though she thanked a higher presence and lifted the gnarled root from the ground.

"Burdock?" Serafina held a plastic bag open as the elderly woman pushed the misshapen root inside.

"Cleans the blood," said Bessie. She tied the bag shut and slung it over her stooped shoulders. "Cold spell's a comin'. We'll need a right smart bunch of these to get us through the winter."

What did you say about belladonna?" Serafina gave Bessie a sideways glance and continued walking. "Did you find belladonna here too?"

"Gather belladonna in the spring. Some people forget. Some people don't know the difference between burdock and belladonna. Easy thing to do. Just have to remember the timing. Timing makes all the difference in the world."

Serafina shrugged. Bessie never answered questions in a straightforward manner.

"Listen." The old woman cupped her hands to her ears and turned in the direction of the house. "Somebody's comin'." Serafina could hear nothing but the sound of a woodpecker hammering the trunk of a nearby tree. But as they parted the thick spruce branches and walked into the clearing behind the old farmhouse, both women could see a blue pickup truck bouncing along the lane down below.

Bessie graced the ground with yet another jet of tobacco juice and cursed under her breath. "What in tarnation are they here for?"

Petey Blue swung the truck to the left to straddle a large rut in the road. He brought the vehicle to a sudden halt near the front porch and switched off the engine. The dust was gently settling over the truck when he popped out of the front door like a vintage jack-in-the-box. He extended his hand to Bessie. She ignored it.

"What do you think you're doing here?" Bessie pointed the shovel at the intruder.

"Greetings and salutations to you, Aunt Bessie. It's your long-lost mountain nephew. You know, me. Petey Blue."

"I reckon I know who you are. T'weren't for me, you'd be just Blue instead of Petey Blue."

"I know. Much obliged for that miraculous rescue on the day of my birth. The episode left me with this bothersome nickname, but that's a small enough price to pay for the joys of being alive."

Marv stepped from the passenger side of the truck. Petey pointed at him. "Me and Marv have come to rescue you now. We heard that your Shep has met with some unfortunate events." Petey Blue cleared his throat and Marv looked at the ground. "I figured that since you stopped me from dying, the least I can do is get your groceries and split you some wood while Shep's…away."

Bessie glared. "Don't need the likes of you two. I can take care of myself. This girl here," she pointed to Serafina, "she gets my groceries and anything else I need. I got enough wood split for winter. You git back over the state line—back on yer side of Feedstone Mountain."

Petey Blue opened his mouth to protest, but Bessie stopped him.

"Listen. Somebody else's a comin'. Reckon this one will be about Shep." The others looked at Bessie as the town police car came into view.

Serafina knew by the look on Jake Preston's face that he hadn't brought good news. Deputy Jason Dove rode shotgun. Not good either. The two lawmen didn't ride together often. One usually stayed in town to deal with day-to-day misadventures in Custer's Mill. She moved closer to Bessie.

Petey Blue was the first to speak as the officers walked toward the little house. "So we meet again, Mr. Policeman. What brings you all the way up here to Jenkins Hollow? Surely not a joy ride."

Jake nodded to the group and then walked over to Bessie and took the old woman's hand. "Can we go inside for a bit? I need to talk to you, and it might be best if you sat down."

Bessie pulled her hand away. Her eyes were cold as steel. "I don't need to sit. What is it? Have they found him? Have they found Shep?

"Yes, ma'am. A young fisherman found his body in the river this morning." He paused. "I'm sorry, ma'am."

Bessie jabbed the shovel into the ground and pulled her shawl tighter around her shoulders. The wind had increased and the air that came from the hollow was a sharp reminder that winter was not far away. "Storm's a-comin'," she said and turned toward the house.

"Go in with her, Dove," said Jake. "See if you can get her to talk. I'll join you in a few minutes."

The young deputy followed the old woman into the house. Jake turned to look out across the valley. From his vantage point at the edge of the hollow, the farms below looked like tiny white dots set in straw colored fields. They seemed to stretch on forever. This must be what was meant by a bird's-eye view. What would it be like to be a bird and soar above it all? Lost in thought, Jake was startled by several loud coughs from the front yard.

"Daydreaming, detective?" Serafina leaned against an ancient oak tree, her long, slender fingers curled around its rough trunk. The late afternoon sun caught her hair at just the perfect angle, highlighting the long auburn strands with iridescent gold. Sometimes Serafina took his breath away. Focus on the job, Preston, he warned himself.

"The view doesn't get much prettier than this," she nodded toward the expanse of evergreens dotted against the royal blue sky. "These mountains are gorgeous." She turned and gave Jake a dazzling smile.

"You got that right," Jake said, his eyes still glued to her hair.

"I meant the trees and the field," she said, and waved a finger as if to remove him from his stupor. And then, as quickly as her smile appeared, it vanished and a cloud settled over her face.

She moved closer and lowered her voice. "What about Shep? You were pretty short on facts when you talked to Bessie. You can cut the gumshoe crap with me. How did he die?"

"Maybe we should go back a bit," Jake said. He plucked a dried blade of grass and crumbled it. "Maybe we should talk about Shep before he was killed. Do you have any idea where he might have been hiding?"

Serafina lowered her eyes. Somewhere in the distance a crow called to its neighbor across the mountain top. "I might. I don't know for sure. Might have. There are a lot of caves around here, you know.

"What gives you the idea Shep stayed in a cave?" He watched her. "You didn't happen to see him, did you?"

Serafina shook her head. "Bessie wouldn't tell me where he was. I'm pretty sure she knew. I'm also pretty sure she left food for him every day. But I don't know that for certain. Bessie is old, but she's crafty. If she has a secret, nobody living will know it unless she chooses to share it."

"Oh? How much do you know about them? The caves, I mean."

"Enough. Some of those caves have pretty good acoustics. A guy I used to date had a punk rock band. They'd practice in the caves sometimes, unplugged. Awesome acoustics."

Jake could hear Dove inside the house as he said his goodbyes to the old lady. He had an idea, but he wasn't sure he wanted to share it with his deputy. Not yet. He leaned toward Serafina. "You interested in showing me around some of these caves one day soon? I could navigate them myself, but it would go much faster if I could go with somebody familiar with the places."

"Why detective, did you just ask me out?"

Jake felt his face turn red. Embarrassed, he picked another blade of grass. "Hardly. I just need a guide," he said. He met her turquoise eyes. "Of course, if it's too much trouble…"

"I'd be honored, sir." She gave him a mock salute. "I'm free Monday. Say about eight? That'll give us time to go to several different caves."

"Sounds good. Meet me at the station? No, on second thought, I'll swing by your shop."

"Do you have a four-wheel drive? Some of those roads are pretty rough."

"I'll bring my truck."

"It's a date, then, detective. I'll pack some sandwiches for lunch."

He watched her stroll across the yard and vanish into the dark woods. "Woodland nymph," he muttered.

"Excuse me, sir?"

He hadn't heard Dove approach.

"Oh nothing. Just mumbling to myself. Any more info from Bessie?"

"No sir. She just closed her eyes and swayed on that old rocker. Sometimes the rocking stopped and she would start to hum. She's a spooky one."

"No kidding. I don't know what kinds of questions she would respond to, but we need to find a way to make her talk to us." The men returned to their car.

"You think she's hiding something, sir?" Dove swung the cruiser around and headed back down the steep, rocky road.

"Yes," said Jake. He winced as a large rock connected with the car's undercarriage. "In fact, she might be the key that solves the whole investigation if only she would talk."

It was about half an hour before time to leave for soccer. Noah Lambert was on the sofa finishing a math assignment when he saw a police car pull into the gravel parking space outside his house. It was the police chief. Why was he here, Noah wondered? Hadn't they covered everything he had to say by the river this morning?

He ran to the kitchen where his mom, Sissy Lambert, stood with her hands in soapy dishwater, washing dishes. His eyes were wide with alarm. "Mom, there's a police car in front of the house."

"Noah, what's the matter? What are you scared of? Chief Preston called and told me he wanted to ask you a few questions about the…about Mr. Crawford and what happened. She dried her hands. "Come on, let's go meet him together."

Noah stood behind his mother as she opened the door and welcomed the police chief into her tidy living room. "Won't you have a seat, Chief Preston?" She smiled and gestured toward the overstuffed chair. "I reckon you're here to talk to Noah. He's been doing his homework and has to leave for soccer in a few minutes." She squeezed Noah's shoulder. "If you don't mind, Chief Preston, I'd like to stay here with you."

"Of course. I'll keep it short, ma'am." Jake smiled. He hoped to reassure Noah that his call was friendly. Noah was nervous. But who wouldn't be after what he'd seen? He wanted the boy to relax.

"Hi there, Noah," said Jake. "How's it going? You hear about that game last weekend? Custer's Mill High showed Blue Hill County who's boss." Jake sat on the edge of the chair and leaned toward the boy.

"Hi, Chief." Noah stood in the doorway and kept his eyes on the floor, wary.

"Noah, I know you have to leave for your game soon, but I'm here to ask you just a couple of questions about this morning. I need to know if you saw or found anything at all around the river bank that might help my investigation."

"That Shep Crawford was a no-account thief." Noah looked straight at Jake now, his brown eyes angry. "That's what my daddy said. So, it's no wonder he's dead."

"Noah." said Sissy. Her tone registered her embarrassment. "That's not how we talk about folks."

"It's true, ma. Everybody says he was a bad guy."

"Well, Noah, even bad folks don't deserve to be killed," said Jake. "And I need your help to find what happened to Mr. Crawford. Was there anything you noticed or saw that might help me?"

Noah's eyes once again focused on the rug. "No, sir. Didn't see nothin' there. Nope. Sorry."

Jake sighed. As he stood to leave, he shook Noah's hand. "Can I give you a ride to the field, Noah? I'd be glad to save you the walk."

"No, thank you sir. I'll walk. Me and my brother Sam like to go over together. He's coming to watch."

Jake watched Sissy's reaction. She was surprised, but said nothing.

"Well, thanks for your time, Mrs. Lambert, Noah. If you think of anything I should know, please call me." He handed Sissy a card with the Custer's Mill police department phone number on it.

"We will, Chief Preston. Won't we Noah?" Sissy turned to her son, but he had already slipped out of the room. She gave Jake a weak smile and held the door open for him.

As Jake returned to his car, he heard Noah calling his brother across the yard. He sat and watched as Sam ran up the hill and joined Noah. They headed down the lane together.

Jake jotted down his impressions in his notebook.

Noah acts spooked. And his mom knows something is off.

Was it the trauma of finding the body?

Is Noah hiding something?

The boy was his best link to the kind of details that solved cases like this. Jake would need to find out more soon.

"Could I give the library some money?" Kate dropped her book bag on the kitchen floor and opened the refrigerator door.

Jake felt comforted by the familiar scene of his kitchen and nearness of his young daughter. His visits with Bessie and Noah had unsettled him. Okay, let's be honest, he thought. Serafina always made him feel unbalanced. It was good to be back in familiar territory.

"Yay! Chocolate milk. Noah Lambert says chocolate milk rots

your teeth." She pulled a cup from the dish drainer beside the sink and filled it with the cavity-producing liquid.

"Whoa. Slow down." Jake Preston took the milk container from his daughter and put the lid back on. "One serving is enough, Kit Kat. You don't want to spoil your dinner. Chicken nuggets and crispy fries."

Kate wrinkled her nose.

"Hey, you said you were tired of hotdogs." Jake smiled. "Now, what did you say about money and the library?"

"This girl at school said that I had a lot of money now, and I should give some away. I think she wanted me to buy her that dumb football poster at the book fair. But I want to give money to the library. They don't have many new books. Maybe I could buy some."

Jake sighed. He had hoped that Kate wouldn't learn about her inheritance from the late Bertha Brubaker for a long time. He should have known better. Living in a small town was similar to living in an aquarium. Everybody saw. Everybody knew.

"It might be a long time before the lawyers take care of all the money issues. They have to sell some of Miss Bertha's things before there will be any money to give out. Miss Bertha had a lot, and she shared it with several different people. But yes, I'm sure you could help the library buy some new books once Mr. Stuart and his co-workers get everything sold. Everything but the old mansion, that is. Miss Bertha wanted the ladies who help at the library to have that."

Kate pulled a tattered book out of her backpack. "Well, we need a new copy of *The Secret Garden*. I checked it out again. Page 67 has a big rip in it, and somebody spilled something on page 235."

"It does look a bit…loved." Jake smiled at his daughter. She looked more like her mother every day: the strawberry blond hair, the earnest blue eyes, and most of all, her caring nature, were all traits of his late wife. Mirabelle would have been so proud.

"Miss Serafina says I can gather herbs with her sometime soon." Kate tucked the shabby copy of her favorite book back into her bag. "Can I go next Saturday?"

"But Saturday is Friends Club at church. Miss Emma will be sad if you don't go." Jake tried to sound casual, but he wasn't at all sure Serafina was a good role model for his Kate to follow.

"I know. I don't think it will matter if I miss one Saturday. Besides, I already know all of the stories they tell and the crafts are boring."

"Kate, that's not a very kind thing to say about Friends Club. You used to love it."

"Yeah, but that was in the summer. When I was still a little kid."

"But you're still seven. You won't be eight until December."

"Could I go with Miss Serafina? Please? Pretty please with honey butter and maple syrup?"

"Let me think about it. Besides, we'll have to see what the weather's like next week."

Regardless of the weather, he had a feeling that spending time with Serafina Wimsey might not be such a stellar idea.

Monday

October 15

Custer's Mill deputy Jason Dove stretched his long legs in front of him, the heels of his polished boots rested on the edge of the metal desk. This was a pose he didn't indulge in often. Not that Chief Preston would mind—he was pretty easy-going when it came to inner office relaxation.

Dove felt so grateful for his job at the town police department. He didn't want to appear to take anything for granted. But the boss was out this morning, combing the caves with that weird Serafina chick, and he had the place to himself.

He picked up a pen and twirled it. Custer's Mill was a quiet place for the most part. That murder at the old Brubaker place this past summer was the most excitement the town had experienced in a long time. Oh well. He enjoyed quiet. Not for him the big city life with gang murders every half hour. Nosiree. He preferred his small-town role to that of an urban policeman any day.

"Uh, Jason?" The quiet voice startled him out of his musing. He put his feet down and wheeled around to face the door.

"Emma. You just about scared the life out of me."

"Sorry. I don't usually have that effect on people. I was just passing by and thought I'd drop Kate's jacket off. She left it at church the other day. Jake around?"

Dove shook his head. "Nah, he's not here this morning."

"Oh? Is he on a call? I see the cruiser is still parked in back."

Dove shifted in his seat. "He took his own truck. Four-wheel drive."

"Really? I didn't think our roads were that bad." Emma draped the jacket across the back of a metal chair.

"Well, he's off-road today."

"Jenkins Hollow?"

"Probably in the vicinity."

"Come on, Jason. He can't be on a secret mission. Give me a clue, for heaven's sake."

"He's looking through some of the caves on North Mountain. He hopes to find evidence that might lead to more information about Shep Crawford's death."

"Well, why didn't you just say so? I'll just catch him another time." Emma started to walk toward the door but turned around. "Wait. Jake's new here. He doesn't know those caves. You let him go alone?"

"Well, not exactly," Dove stammered. "He does have a guide."

"Who?" The single word was filled with meaning.

Dove sighed. There was no way out of this. "Serafina Wimsey. She grew up around here. She knows those caves backward and forward."

Emma stood still. In the back of the room, a scanner beeped and a crackled voice gave directions to an accident in Mill City.

"I didn't mean to upset you, Emma. But you asked. And she does know the caves."

"That's because she has no concept of fear. She's the golden child. Nothing can hurt her. Do you know when we were kids she wanted to play hide-n-seek in those caves?"

Dove smiled. "Bet your parents wouldn't have been too happy with that idea."

"My dad would have nailed my hide to the wall. But Serafina's mom could have cared less. She wasn't even at home most nights."

Emma glanced at the clock. "Guess it's no use for me to wait here for Jake. He could be gone all day."

"I'll give him the jacket and tell him you dropped by." Dove held the office door open for her.

"No, don't tell him I was here. Just tell him something about the jacket. I don't care what."

Dove sighed as he heard her car pull away. Women. He'd never understand them. Not in a million years.

"Well that was a bust. The next cave we'll check is just a few miles further up the mountain." Serafina gestured to the steep grade in front of them. "Probably take us ten minutes from here, as long as the road is clear. Hope you have a chain saw in the back. You need one sometimes, out this way." She looked over at Jake, her turquoise eyes sparkling. "This is fun."

Jake shook his head. "Nope, no chain saw, I'm afraid. If we get caught on the mountain, I'll have to call Dove to come help."

"Hah. You won't get a signal out here. Unless you're on one of those peaks, maybe." Serafina looked at the sky, where clouds had darkened the sunlight off to the northwest. He supposed there must be mountaintops behind the clouds, but they were hidden. She laughed and began to hum a mournful tune Jake had never heard.

Jake shook his head. This woman was different from any girls he'd known. She made him feel slightly off-kilter and stupid. Like she knew tantalizing secrets he didn't know. But the cave they'd just left showed no sign of anyone camping there. No sign of Shep Crawford.

He hoped the next stop would make this jaunt worthwhile. Why didn't he bring Dove along? Serafina had insisted she could show him at least four caves, and he'd just gone along with her. Like a dumb sheep. What kind of spell had she cast on him, anyhow?

Serafina directed Jake to a series of turns. The road, if you could call it that, had become narrow and rocky. Jake's truck lurched along as he tried to avoid the largest potholes. Serafina whooped when she bounced so high she almost hit her head on the ceiling, shoulder straps notwithstanding.

"This is my kind of ride, Jake. Now just past that outcropping there. You'll be able to park kind of off the road. But we'll have to walk from there. It's too steep, even for your four-wheel drive manly-man truck."

Jake climbed out of the cab. "Lead on, Sacajawea. I'm at your mercy."

"Ooh, I like the sound of that." She turned toward the woods. "Well, come on, it's not far, but it's a steep trail, and it's not very well-traveled."

The leaves on the trees around them were shades of bright orange, yellow and scarlet as they headed into the woods. As soon as they stepped inside the cloister of trees and undergrowth, sunlight became muted and Jake felt the temperature drop. After a few minutes, he started to feel winded. Serafina was right. It *was* a very steep path.

Serafina seemed to float along like a deer and she kept up a steady pace. Wild blackberry vines grabbed at their jackets as they made their way along the almost invisible trail that showed very little evidence of recent use.

The trail soon disappeared into a mass of tall oak trees. Jake was relieved to see the sun peeking through the clouds. Not a great time for a storm. It was slippery enough walking on leaf-covered rocks without rain to make them treacherous.

Serafina motioned to Jake. "Here it is. Just under that flat rock."

She ducked low and disappeared into the crevice. Jake followed, hitting his head on an overhang in the process. I must be insane to come here with this wild woman. What happened to my sensible police training?

As they entered the cave, he stopped and waited. His eyes were slow to adjust to the darkness. He played his flashlight over the low rock ledge ahead of them. The space opened into a chamber where he could stand to his full height.

Serafina motioned with her own flashlight and he followed her around a corner. They squeezed through another passage, then sidestepped along a ledge to a gap in the rock. Jake wondered how far the drop would be if they slipped.

"Please be careful, Serafina." A waver in his voice betrayed him.

He wondered who he was warning, anyway. Not Miss Mountain Woman, that was certain.

The ground sloped downward and Jake hesitated. Well, here goes, he thought. I'm all in.

But the next chamber they entered was large and his light caught a glint of metal. Then another. Cans of baked beans, corn and peaches were scattered in disarray along the far wall, and a dark blanket roll lay next to a large irregular discoloration on the smooth cave floor. He moved closer.

"That's blood, if I'm not mistaken," he said, his voice hushed in the still air." He bent down to scrape a sample, and sealed it in a plastic bag. "Could be Shep's blood. We'll have to see. This is a snug hideout."

Jake flipped his flashlight beam back to Serafina's face. She was pale, with an uncharacteristic look of fear. Was it the sight of the bloodstain that shocked her, or did she know something she hadn't told him?

"Sorry you had to see this, Serafina. C'mon. Let's get out of here and go back to the truck." He took her elbow and guided her toward the opening of the chamber.

Jake felt uneasy as he secured the opening to the cave with police tape. He needed an officer here as soon as possible to stand watch until he could get a full forensics team on the site. The wind had picked up and the sun had disappeared again behind heavy gray clouds.

Jake and Serafina hiked back along the rocky path in silence.

The first lash of rain hit as they arrived at the truck. Jake pulled back onto the roadway just as the skies opened and delivered a terrific deluge. The road became almost invisible in the downpour, and as the truck bounced down the mountain, they hit potholes now filled with water.

"Whew, great driving, Jake." Serafina held on to the ceiling handle, laughing as they lurched and splashed along.

A split second later, the truck hit a deep pothole on a sharp curve. The slick surface defied Jake's attempt to guide it back to the center of the road. They veered off the shoulder and over several low-lying bushes before a large oak tree brought the truck to an abrupt halt with a dull thump. The airbags inflated, and threw them back against the seats.

It was quiet for a moment inside the truck. Water hissed from the radiator. In seconds, the airbags deflated. Jake's face stung from the bag's impact.

"Are you okay, Serafina? Jake grabbed her arm, his face full of alarm. "What an idiot." He pounded his hands on the steering wheel. "I am so sorry."

"Well, that airbag smacked me good. It smarts and I feel dizzy." Serafina put her hand to her head. It felt moist and sticky.

"You're bleeding, Serafina." Jake opened the glove compartment and took out some napkins. "Here, use these to wipe your face. There should be a first-aid kit in here too." He rummaged behind the seat and found a box with bandages and ointments.

"There's still a little ice in my water bottle. I'll put it in this cloth bandage, and you should hold it on your eye."

Serafina pulled down the mirror to inspect the damage. Her nose bled and her left eye was already swollen. She pinched her nostrils to apply pressure, and held the ice pack over her eye with her other hand.

"I'm afraid you'll end up with a black eye." He touched her forehead gently with his fingers. "How are you now? Let's see if the bleeding has stopped."

"I think it's stopped," she said. "I'll be okay. We mountain women are tough, you know."

"But I feel terrible. I should never have asked you to come on this investigation."

"I forgive you. But you owe me a real date now." Serafina gave Jake's hand a squeeze.

"You know any place nearby where I can make a call?" he asked.

"The Fulks live about a half-mile or so down this road on the right. I can find it. We'll have to wade across the river to get to their place."

"With that eye, you need to stay put. Let me go." Jake studied Serafina as he tried to assess her true condition. "You sure you're okay?"

"I'll be fine. I'll just sit here with my icepack and enjoy the storm. Look for the lane—it's just past the bridge. And it's long, maybe a quarter mile or more. Be careful with all this rain. Flash floods are pretty common up here."

"What about this road? Might it flood, too?"

"We're on high ground here, and the river's pretty far below us. I've never known this part of the mountain to flood."

"Okay, I'll be back as soon as I've called for help." Jake zipped his jacket as high as it would go, hopped out, and in seconds had disappeared into the pouring rain.

The wind whipped around Jake. The rain lashed at his body. He was in trouble and so was Serafina, thanks to him. Water rushed in rivulets down the mountain road, making it hard to avoid the potholes and mudslides.

How could he have been so careless? Jake had questioned his judgment over a dozen times today. What a mistake he had made when he left Jason back at the police station. In fact, he should never have involved Serafina at all. Dove knew the caves as well as she did. He pounded his thigh as a violent gust stung his face with rain and he gave an agonized cry of frustration.

The realization that Serafina had manipulated the situation hit him hard. Now they were both stuck on this mountain in the storm. She was hurt, and his truck was disabled. Their cell phones? Useless. At least, he thought, Serafina is safe in the truck. He hoped, at least. She wouldn't try to go anywhere by herself, would she? He felt sick.

Fighting the wind and the rain, Jake felt like he'd walked for miles already. He couldn't remember when he'd felt so helpless and vulnerable. Maybe when Mirabelle died, but back then, he had to stay strong for Kate.

Fear gripped him. What about Kate? If something happened to him, who would take care of her? Both of his parents were gone. Mirabelle's mother had died in the house fire years ago. Jake thought now how Kate's newfound relationship to the Brubaker family had changed their lives forever. Her inheritance was more money than Jake had ever dreamed about. He worried that Kate might be susceptible to those unsavory and unscrupulous people who prey upon innocents.

Jake was sobered by the realization that other than himself, Billy Brubaker was Kate's only living relative. Surely, no person in his right mind would leave a young child like Kate under Billy's care, a man of questionable character.

Jake shook himself. Steady, boy. This sense of imminent danger caused his imagination to run away with him.

His feet slipped on some wet leaves, and he came down hard on his right knee. He tried to break the fall by bracing his hands in front of him. The stones cut into his palms. Jake caught his breath and struggled to stand. A red stain spread across the torn knee of his trousers. His hands bled.

The rain came down harder. It took all of his strength to keep upright and move forward against the force of the torrent.

Serafina had told him the Fulk's place would be on the right, about half mile from where the truck hit the tree. He lifted his head, and held his arm up to shield his eyes from the rain. "No." he groaned.

Down the road, he saw the one-lane bridge. Roiling water already poured over the wooden planks. Tree branches and chunks of roots raced down the swollen river bed. Jake moved off the road and into the woods. He'd try to cross the stream above the bridge.

The blanket of colorful leaves he'd admired earlier today, now made the forest floor treacherous. As he got closer to the stream, he noticed large boulders of rock jutting in all directions. Jake had to concentrate on each step he took.

The water was cold. Jake gasped. He struggled against the strong current that pulled at his legs and body. He tried to hold onto the rocks. If the water pulled him under, it would sweep him downstream.

Jake's mind went to Emma, and an image of Kate and Emma walking hand-in-hand at Nanette's pumpkin patch. As Kate had said, they seemed like a family that day.

You've done it again Preston. He felt a stab of anger at himself. Emma was sure to be upset when she heard he'd come here with Serafina. He needed to talk with her and straighten things out.

Jake pushed forward, taking the final steps to reach the opposite streambank. Pulling himself out of the water, he could see a rough-hewn path through the trees. It gave way to a clearing. He could see only the shadowy outline of several buildings through the rain. He heard a couple of dogs barking and hoped they were behind a fence. Or at least tied to a sturdy oak.

Jake could make out the silhouette of a stooped figure on the porch. He wasn't sure if country etiquette required a "halloo" or a "howdy." A flash of lightning revealed that he'd better soon make up his mind. The stooped figure held a rifle.

"Howdy sir? Mr. Fulk?" Jake limped toward the house with his palms up.

The old man spat as lightning once again lit the sky. "Mebee I am. Mebee I ain't. What's it to ya?"

"My truck got stuck a ways back. I wondered if I could use your phone to call for help?" Jake put a weary hand on the porch railing, water trickling down his face and into his eyes. Inside the house he heard the snarls and growls again. He hoped the phone was mobile and he could use handset on the porch.

"I don't know ya from Adam. How if you're a killer? How if you come to take my money. Mebee even the old pump organ my granny left me." The man sneered at Jake.

"If you'll let me stand on the porch out of the rain, I can show you my ID. I'm Chief of Police at Custer's Mill. Jake Preston."

The old man rubbed the stubble on his chin. "Ya don't say. Well, I reckon Susie can take care of you're lyin', or if you mean us harm." He motioned to the screen door and Jake could see a drooling pit bull. "C'mon then."

Jake stood under the tin roof of the porch, grateful to be out of the rain. He pulled out his wallet and held his police ID toward the man.

He glanced at Jake and nodded. "I reckon you can come in. Watch your step."

Jake walked into a tiny room lit by a bug-spattered 40-watt bulb. The pit bull, on command from her master, hunched in the corner with a wary eye on Jake's every movement. A scrawny Chihuahua nipped at his heels, and an ancient beagle raised a rheumy eye but didn't move or make a sound. "Thank you so much. Where's the phone, Mr. Fulk. You are Mr. Fulk, right?"

The man nodded. "Call me Clay. Short for Clarence. Used to call me Clare, but that name belongs to a woman. And I ain't no woman." He sniggered and pointed to a dark corner.

There on a rickety shelf was a rotary dial phone. So much for talking on the porch. But the dogs seemed under control, and Jake held the receiver and watched the wheel spin.

"Hello, Custer's Mill Police Department. Dove here."

"Dove." Jake felt relief flood over him as he heard the young officer's voice. "We're stuck here on North Mountain." He gave directions to Dove. "My truck slid off the road, and I need Ed with his tow-truck to get us back to town.

Jake turned his back on his host and lowered his voice. "But first, I need you to call for a forensics team to get here as soon as the roads are passable. I'll fill you in when I get back."

"And Dove, one more thing. Can you call Emma and ask her to get Kate from day care for me? I need to know she is safe."

Dove hesitated before he spoke. "Ah, sir, I think she might be a bit upset with you right now. She came by this morning. When I told her you were looking through the caves, she kind of figured you were with Serafina."

Jake moaned. "I'd hoped that was something I could tell her myself. Well, I'm sure Emma will take care of Kate. Just tell her I need to talk with her as soon as possible. As soon as you can get me off this mountain, Dove. Hurry."

Emma's cell phone buzzed in her pocket just as she shut down her computer for the afternoon. She looked at the number. The Custer's Mill police department. Now maybe she was getting somewhere.

"Jake?" She tried not to sound too eager.

"No. Sorry. This is Dove."

"Oh. Hi Jason." Her voice was flat.

Dove hesitated. "Um. Emma? The boss called. He got stuck in the mountains in the storm. He was wondering if you could get Kate from her after-school program?"

"He got stuck on the mountain with *Serafina?*" Emma began to pace the floor.

Dove cleared his throat. "Well, yes. I suppose so. Anyway, he wondered if you could pick up Kate from her after-school program? I think it's over soon."

Emma's first instinct was to refuse. Who did he think he was anyway? A member of royalty? Better yet, who did he think *she* was? His loyal servant? Still, she loved Kate, and the child shouldn't have to suffer just because her father acted like a jerk.

She sighed. "Of course. I'll get her. And you can tell him," she said, as she paused to let the sarcasm soak in, "when it's convenient for him, he can stop by to get his daughter. After his fun date."

Dove sounded both relieved and embarrassed. "Thanks, Emma. I'm sure it will ease his mind to know that you're taking care of Kate."

"Of course," Emma mumbled. "It's what I live for—easing Jake's mind."

Nothing at the Spare Change Diner was what it seemed. The menus were in French, but no French food other than french fries was on the menu. The floor boards looked like vintage barn planks, but the moment a spike heel came in contact with the surface, the resulting dent on the slat showed the flooring to be made of soft vinyl. The counters and tabletops were faux marble, and the silverware was stainless steel in a variety of patterns.

Back when the diner opened in the late 40s, Edward Thompson had just returned from a stint in World War II. He'd been based in France near the Riviera, and had become enamored with all things Parisian. His goal, when he returned to the United States, was to create a charming French bistro, an elegant restaurant that mirrored his favorite eating spots in France.

It didn't take long for him to learn that the folks of Custer's Mill had not developed a taste for escargot and coq au vin. They had no patience to wait for the 7-hour leg of lamb, and provincial onion tarts were not to their liking.

But he'd already spent a lot of money printing menus, and he wasn't about to scrap these expensive items and start from scratch. So he adapted the food to fit the menus. Escargot meant deep fried clam strips, coq au vin translated into chicken patty sandwiches, and onion tarts were onion rings. In time, the folks at Custer's Mill got so used to the French menus that they protested when Mr. Thompson's grandson, Junior, tried to change the list of food options to be more accurate.

Customers saw subtle changes to the decor. Junior washed grease stains from the floral wallpaper. He replaced the old window coverings with more modern mini-blinds, and added bright new blue gingham tablecloths over the chipped table tops. He sanded and repainted the bar stools that had become faded over years of customers' use.

The one concession he made to his grandfather was to serve café au lait. Plain, strong coffee with a touch of thick, fresh cream. The Spare Change Diner was famous for its café au lait. The folks in Custer's Mill even learned how to say it. Sort of.

The people gathered at the diner today were the usual lot plus a few more. The whole town reeled with the news of the discovery of Shep Crawford's body in the North Fork.

"I think," said Laurence George, as he wound a fettuccini noodle around his fork, "that justice is always served. In one way or another. That Crawford man broke the law and now he's paid for it. Paid dearly, I admit, but still, one can't hope to go through life tempting fate and getting away with it."

"I think," said Nanette Steele, swiveling on the bar stool to look Laurence straight in the eye, "that you are a pompous ass. Nobody deserves to be murdered."

"Now wait a minute," said Jane, "we don't know that Shep was murdered. They've only just found his body. There hasn't been time to make an official statement."

"You know as well as I do that bodies don't just find their way into the river on their own. Especially a body with a couple of rocks tied to it," said Laurence.

"That's just hearsay." Jane added a pack of sugar to her iced tea and stirred. "I prefer to give my verdict when Dr. Atkins releases the official medical examiner's report. What do you think, Emma? You've been quiet this evening."

"Just exhausted."

"That's why you get the big bucks, my dear," said Laurence with a smirk. "But stop thinking about your own weariness for a minute and give us your opinion on this body they found."

Emma sighed. "You mean Shep, Laurence? He has a name, you know. And I'm with Jane. It's too early to make an educated guess."

"Well, if you're that snippy with the patrons at your library, it's no wonder that my bookstore has more customers." Laurence leaned back and stared at Emma through half-closed eyes. He turned his gaze toward the diner door and his face grew pale.

"See a ghost, Laurence?" Nanette waved her hand in front of his face. "Hey. Wake up. Are you frozen?"

At that moment, the door opened and in swept a young Cary Grant—or at least that's how Nanette was to describe him later.

"Alex?" Laurence's voice was tight and its pitch seemed to have increased an octave or more.

"In the flesh, dear brother." The man smiled.

"But I thought…"

"I can imagine what you thought, and none of it's good." Alex put his hand on his brother's shoulder. "By the way, I just passed the family store and noticed you've changed the name. Bard's Nest? What happened to George's Art, Antiques and Jewelry?"

Laurence still looked shell-shocked, but his voice had returned to its normal pitch. "When you left after Father's funeral, without even a good-bye, I figured you were finished with the lot. Family, antiques, the shop."

"Well, you figured wrong, dear brother. I'm back. And I suspect we may just make a few tweaks to the store."

"Now," he said, as he turned toward the rest of the group, "Please forgive me for airing our family's dirty laundry. I promise to behave better in the future."

As usual, Nanette was the first to find her voice. "Well if it's not young Alex. Come on over here to the light, boy. Let me get a good look at you." Alex winked at her and walked over to the hanging lamp above the bar.

"Well, well, well. You clean up pretty nice, young man. I think the last time I saw you, you had a black eye and a bloody cheek. That was…what? Twenty-five years ago now?"

"What was I, fourteen?" asked Alex. "I think Buster Archer deserved that punch. Not sure I deserved the wallop his brother gave me though."

"Wasn't long after that you got sent to that boarding school. Where was it? Boston?"

"The Bentley School for Boys. Wellingsley, Massachusetts. The Hall of Academic Horrors."

"But that's where Father…" Laurence's face was now bright red. "It was an honor for you to go. You were lucky Aunt Betsy's legacy was enough to put you through school. What I would have given…" His voice trailed off.

"You don't need charm school, brother mine. You have an aura of charisma all your own."

"Is that what they call it nowadays?" Nanette said.

Laurence appeared to have regained some of his composure. "Sit down, Alex. Have a cup of coffee on me and tell us about this surprise visit."

"You are most generous." Alex sat down beside his brother. "And as to why I'm here, I think I've made myself clear. I'm ready to resurrect the family business. And of course, he added, as he winked at Emma, 'I've missed the beauty of the ladies who inhabit this little burg. And the wisdom of its elders." He glanced at Nanette.

"Still full of navy beans, I see," said Nanette.

Laurence tore open a pack of artificial sweetener and poured it into his coffee. "I thought you understood, Alex. The antique store went out of business a while back. Just not enough demand for old things in Custer's Mill. Most people still use their antiques. Butcher-block tables, oil lamps, pie safes. They inherited the lot from their parents and grandparents. They don't need to buy any more."

"So, you just made the decision to close the store? On your own?"

"Give me a break, Alex. You left town without a trace. I didn't know where to find you to talk it over."

"Fair enough." Alex stretched his legs into the aisle of the diner, and almost tripped a waitress carrying a tray of drinks. "Oops, sorry ma'am." The waitress frowned. She took a second look and gave him a tentative smile. "But I'm back now. Back and ready to peddle my wares."

"But I have a good business as a book seller. Tourists enjoy the store when they pass through." Laurence was agitated.

"Well, I don't want to overthrow your literary kingdom, dear brother. I see we are not compatible. Although why that should surprise me I don't know. Tell you what. We'll share your precious bookstore. You sell books. I'll sell antiques. I can use our old warehouse for shipments I have arriving. Soon."

Laurence looked doubtful. "I'm not sure that would work. I've already rented out spaces in that building. Serafina Wimsey opened an herb shop on one end."

"I think Miss Wimsey and I would be quite compatible. In fact, if she's that gorgeous ginger I've glimpsed in town, I'd say we'll be more than compatible. She was just a scrawny brat last time I saw her," Alex said. "But you know what, brother, we don't have to discuss our business plans now in front of these venerable folks. I have work to do."

Laurence shifted in his chair. "Just one more thing. Where do you plan to stay while you're here?"

For the first time since his grand entrance, Alex looked uneasy. "I've booked a couple nights in a hotel in Mill City. I thought maybe you'd put me up for a bit, bro. You live in that big mausoleum by yourself, don't you?"

"I wouldn't call our ancestral home a mausoleum."

"Well it's too big for just one person. Maybe I can take my old room back."

"How long do you plan stay around?"

"I told you. I'm here to help revive the family business. And we do need to discuss this later." Alex glanced down the bar. "Why, I see my middle school science teacher. Ms. Allman, how in the world are you?" Alex slid off the bar stool, gave it a spin, and walked over to stand behind Jane.

"I'm not teaching anymore. But I remember you were quite the scientist in eighth grade. You were in my last middle school class before I moved over to the high school."

"We both switched schools the same year. How did you like high school, Ms. Allman?"

"Ah, but you're the subject now, Alex. Did you go any further with your science interests?"

"I'm afraid our esteemed Boys Academy didn't do much with science. It was more of an art school."

"Did you turn out to be an artist?" asked Nanette.

"Of sorts," said Alex. "I attended the Academy of Arts in

California. My degree in Interior Architecture and Design gave me an excuse to wander through some of the most prestigious auction houses in the world. For the past seven years, I've worked in Europe. That's pretty much been my life for the past while." He paused. "What's been going on in this town for the last couple decades?"

"Well, our town is about to be put on the national historical registry," said Marguerite. "Seems our library here has some historical significance."

"And of course, there's the dead body they just found floating in the river," Nanette said.

"Dead body?" Alex brushed a tiny lock of hair from his forehead. "Well, well, well. Murder comes to Custer's Mill. What a change of pace for you."

"Not really. And no one said it was murder," said Jane. "The verdict is still out."

Serafina had taken the long way down to the warehouse. After the harrowing experience with Jake in the mountains earlier that afternoon, she needed some time to walk and unwind. The incident had disturbed her to say the least. And not just because they almost nosedived down the side of the mountain.

The storm was over now, and calm surrounded Custer's Mill—the kind of tranquil almost eerie serenity that sometimes descends following one of nature's turbulent performances. Water still gurgled through the drainpipes at a steady pace. Tree branches were down here and there, and wet leaves covered the sidewalks.

Serafina shook the water droplets from her umbrella and left it on the front stoop to dry. The swelling in her face had gone down, but she had an impressive-looking shiner from the airbag.

A steady staccato of droplets bounced off the granite counter and onto the floor, and Serafina heard it as soon as she opened the door. There was a hole in the roof. That much was evident. A branch had fallen from the enormous oak tree that covered her end of the warehouse and poked through beams high above the back of her shop. Water from the perennially clogged downspout trickled through a split in the sheet metal roofing and onto her counter. A quick check around the shop assured her that moisture had not yet damaged any merchandise. She'd have to call Laurence and have him repair the roof. Fast.

She reached for the phone and stopped. There had been a truck parked at the side of the warehouse. Maybe someone there could lend a hand. If she could just get a sheet of plastic over that hole tonight.

The corridor that connected the two rooms of the aging cinderblock warehouse was dark and musty. She could hear scraping sounds at the other end of the building. She hoped someone could help her pull the branch off the roof.

"Yoo-hoo. Anybody home?" She entered the dim shop and saw a man dressed in a dark hoodie and grey sweatpants, bending over a wooden crate. He looked a bit familiar, but she couldn't quite place him.

"Why it's the friendly neighborhood herbalist." Alex George flashed Serafina a gleaming smile. Then he started as his eyes registered on her bruises. "What in the world happened to your face?"

"Just a little run-in with an airbag. And my name's Serafina. Serafina Wimsey at your service." She curtseyed, then extended her hand.

"Why, I believe I remember you from when you were a little girl. I'm Alex George, and I'm your new warehouse neighbor. Very nice to see you again. If you look this good with a busted face, I can't imagine what you'll be like when it all heals."

He was good looking, that was a fact. Serafina wondered if he had money as well. Looks were nice, but rather useless when it came to paying the rent. She had learned that fact quite early in life. Not one of the series of handsome men that clustered around her mom had a dollar to spare. They would stay a few weeks, usually until the rent was due—and then disappear.

"What are you doing here so late?" Serafina looked at her watch and then at Alex.

"I could ask you the same question," said Alex.

"I came over to see if the storm did any damage this afternoon. Looks like a branch blew down and punched a hole in my shop roof. It's dripping on my counter. I suppose it would be too much to hope that you have a ladder here?"

He shook his head. "Afraid not. But tell you what. I can get my brother over here first thing in the morning. I don't think it's going to rain anymore tonight."

"Bet he'll be thrilled."

"Oh, Laurence is a big, grumpy teddy bear. He'll grumble a bit, but he'll have Hoyt Miller's nephew up there patching your roof first thing in the morning."

Serafina looked around at the sealed crates. "What's in those?"

"A cedar chest," said Alex.

"Are these all cedar chests?" She pointed to the stacks of crates lining the room.

"Oh no. I deal mostly in antiques from estate sales. I've got all kinds of stuff in here."

"Sounds interesting. I'd like to see more of what you've got some time."

"I'll make sure that happens," he winked.

"In the meantime, I'd appreciate it if you would remember to tell Laurence about the roof," said Serafina as she turned to go. "I don't think it's a huge repair, probably just a patch over that metal roof. I was afraid there might be more damage than that. The wind must have been worse on the mountain."

"Oh?" Alex raised an eyebrow. "What were you doing on a mountain?"

"I can't possibly see how that is any of your business, but let's just say that I had a somewhat perilous adventure with our new town police chief on North Mountain today."

"So what'd he do? Deputize you and send you on a wild goose chase?"

"Not as wild as you might think. I'd say we had a profitable day."

Alex dropped the crowbar he was using to wedge the top off the smallest crate. "How so?"

"Hey, I shouldn't have said anything, okay? Leave it alone."

"Methinks the lady doth protest too much." Alex rested his foot on top of a crate and leaned over, chin in hand. A perfect pose of suave masculinity.

"All of that and Shakespeare too." Serafina frowned and turned once more to leave. "Just remember how things turned out for Hamlet."

"Not to mention Ophelia."

"I'll expect the roof repairman first thing in the morning then, Alex," she called over her shoulder.

"First thing, ma'am." He gave her a mock salute and returned to his work.

Tuesday

October 16

It was just past sunrise the next morning when Jake left the town manager's office. He'd explained the discovery of the cave and the ensuing truck wreck. The town manager was unhappy with him for failing to take Dove along, and had questioned his relationship with Serafina.

He was right. Jake should have waited until his deputy could come with him. It was an embarrassing situation and he'd been unprofessional. It wouldn't happen again.

Dove was on the phone when Jake reached his office. He motioned to get the call over with. They had to return to the cave as soon as possible. And they'd take the police jeep this time.

"Bring a pack with you, Dove." Jake's voice was terse. "I'll need you to stay on the scene until I can get other backup there to help. You'll need some gear."

"Yes, sir." Dove pulled the pack from the storage closet and jogged to keep up with Jake as he headed to the parking lot.

Despite his youth, Dove was wise enough to know his boss was in no mood for chatter. The men drove through Custer's Mill and onto the mountain roads in silence. Their journey was interrupted by a few radio transmissions before they lost coverage. The road was bumpy and slick. It was in worse shape now since the downpour.

Dove was relieved when Jake finally pulled over. He jumped out of the jeep and shrugged the backpack on.

Jake pointed to a faint but muddy trail behind some wild blackberry vines. "Up here. We'll have to take it easy if we want to get there in one piece."

Headway was slow over the slippery rocks. The rain had washed away sections of the trail, and showers of water drenched them as they made occasional detours through the wet foliage.

Just before they reached the mouth of cave, Jake stopped short. Dove almost bumped into him. "Wait a minute." Jake pointed to footprints that led into the cave. "These are new." The yellow police tape sagged low across the bushes where Jake had tied it. "And the tape has been disturbed."

He crouched low to inspect the marks in the mud before he took several photos with his phone and bagged a sample of the soil. "Someone's been here and they went inside. C'mon, Dove. Let's see if he's still in here."

Dove set the backpack down behind a boulder. The men pulled out their service revolvers and flipped on their flashlights. As they eased inside, excitement and fear gave them both a sudden adrenaline rush. Balancing with their elbows against the rock wall, they made their way through the passages. If someone was still inside, he could be dangerous and armed. And he would have the advantage.

Jake led the way in silence toward the chamber where he and Serafina had found the blood and the tin cans. He flicked his light ahead as he watched for any sign of movement. Sounds of dripping water and their own heavy breathing seemed too loud in their ears as they strained to hear anything that indicated another person nearby. Waiting. Maybe watching them.

They entered the chamber and hugged the left wall. Jake was on high alert. He motioned to Dove to step in and cover the right side. The two circled the room, revolvers aloft and lights shining on walls and floor.

The dark red stain was on Dove's side and he shone his light on it. "No one seems to be here, sir. I see that blood stain, though."

"Yeah, I've already sent a sample of that off to the lab. But these cans were all over the floor when I was here earlier." Jake pointed to the food cans, now rolled against the far wall." And that messy pile of blankets was folded then. Somebody's been here. Looking for something. And they're either gone already or listening to us right now."

Dove had moved around a large boulder which led into the next chamber. He bent over and stuck his head through the opening. "I'll check around in here real quick, sir."

Dove's light played on a rock ledge at the top of the cave. He felt along the surface. His hand struck a cold object and he pulled back, surprised. "Sir," he called to Jake. "There's something here. A gun of some kind."

Jake moved as fast as he could without whacking his forehead on the low opening. He emerged into the chamber where they were both able to stand at full height. "Up there, sir—don't want to touch it again. I have a bag here to put it in."

Dove stood on his toes and lifted the gun from the ledge. He took care to hold it only with the handkerchief he'd pulled from his pocket. "It's a beauty, sir. And it's heavy."

He handed the bag to Jake. It was heavy. Even in the dim light, Jake could see the long barrel and extensive engraving in gold and silver.

Jake whistled. "Wow, this is an antique revolver. Looks like a very rare one. I've only seen pistols like this in museums or private collections. We'll have to get it analyzed and checked for prints. And see if a gun collector is missing one of these."

He tucked the bag inside his jacket and its bulky shape made a bulge on his side.

"Now let's check that ledge one more time, Dove."

The two men felt along the ledge, working their way to the center. Jake's hand hit a small soft object. It was a string-tied leather bag. He placed it in an evidence bag and worked it open. Gold and silver coins. Old ones. He drew in his breath.

"Looks like Shep may have been involved in some kind of fencing operation." Dove said.

"Sure does. Now let's get back outside. I want you to stay here and guard the entrance. I'll call the county and ask them to send someone over to relieve you, and to help us search this cave. I want this site secure until we've got all the information we need."

"Yes, sir."

"And I'll be back in a couple of hours, too. I want to check the road for tire marks or any other sign of how somebody got here."

Outside the cave, Dove moved his pack to the top of a rock outcropping and began to prepare for his vigil. "I'll be here, sir. With my gun drawn, just in case."

"Be careful and be very alert. I'll see you soon."

Jake slid and slithered down the path as fast as he could. He arrived at the jeep with thick mud caked on his boots. He looked around for tire marks and was rewarded with a deep impression of a tire about twenty feet from where he had pulled over.

The tread was clearly visible. He placed a sample of the mud from the tracks in an evidence bag and took a picture of the tread with his phone. Forensics could make a cast if they got here before another rainstorm.

Okay, friend, Jake thought, his face grim. We're gonna find you. You can be sure of that.

Sunday
October 21

The sun had begun to dip behind the tip of Shenandoah Mountain by the time Emma settled on her back porch with a cup of chamomile tea. All day she had shoved thoughts of Shep and the recovery of his body to the back of her mind. Now that the day was done and chores finished, the silence forced her to go back to an issue that she had never quite resolved, an uncomfortable twist of thoughts that she knew needed to be untangled. Shep's death brought it all back.

Part of her was glad that justice had been served. Shep was wanted for murder, and now he had been killed. An eye for an eye, as Hiram often said. But if justice was all there was, why did she feel sad? Why did she wish with all her heart that she could turn back time? Why did she wish that Shep was still alive, and that he was still just a strange man who followed orders like a marionette on a string?

Her cat, Molasses, jumped on her lap, bumped the teacup and spilled tea down the side and onto Emma's lap. Emma set the cup down. She cuddled him close to her face, taking in the scent of lavender on his fur. Molasses had been chasing bumblebees again. It was a mystery to Emma why he never got stung when he so often disturbed the bees daily labor. Justice didn't always happen.

She still had nightmares about being chased through a narrow tunnel. Funny though, it was never former Police Chief Pete Anderson who was after her. Not like it had been in real life. It was always a dragon. A fire-breathing dragon. Perhaps that recurring dream had more to do with the fire in the vault instead of the person who set it. Maybe it was fire. The fire that killed Eric. She ought to see a therapist and work through this snarl of feelings and emotions.

Billy Brubaker sat on a flimsy wire chair that was squeezed among the boxes on his tiny deck. He didn't look forward to unpacking. In fact, he'd just as soon toss it all and start over.

Trouble was, he had no money. You couldn't start over unless you had a decent source of income. He'd had to sell the fancy house to pay court costs after he'd been indicted as an accessory to attempted murder. It was Pete Anderson's fault. He'd been blackmailing Billy for all those years.

Billy knew he should be grateful he'd gotten off with only community service. Still, he'd lost almost everything. He'd lost his job as Custer's Mill town manager. And over half of his rightful inheritance was going to Kate Preston. He'd also lost what respect he'd had from the citizens of Custer's Mill. At least he'd have some money again when they sold Aunt Bertha's holdings and he'd gotten his share from the lawyer.

Folks kept telling him he needed to work hard to rebuild their trust. It made him weary. He doubted anyone would ever take him seriously again. It was wrong, he knew, but he almost envied Shep. The guy was dead. Nobody expected a dead guy to reform. And the police would never know for sure if it was Shep who poisoned Bertha Brubaker and almost killed Hiram Steinbacher.

Billy tore a crust from his ham sandwich and tossed it into the air. A grackle swooped down and caught it before it hit the ground. So his life had come to this. He fed the birds and collected road trash. Not much else. He wondered if anyone would bother to question him about Shep's death. He hoped they wouldn't. Billy wanted to erase the grisly past he shared with the man.

Monday

October 22

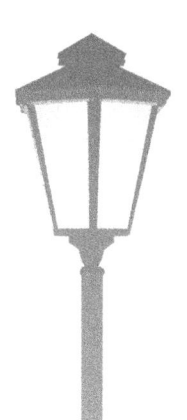

"Make yourself at home, my dear. There's more coffee in the pot. And if you'd rather have tea, I can heat some water in the kettle. I can have it ready in a jiffy." Jane Allman glanced at her niece who absent-mindedly twirled a spoon on the glossy wooden surface of the kitchen table.

"Oh, don't fuss, Aunt Jane. I'm fine."

'Fine' was not a word Jane would have chosen to describe her niece at the moment. The younger woman abandoned the spoon and now sat cradling her coffee cup as she stared into space. Her long, brown hair was twisted into a loose knot at the back of her neck, and her flannel nightgown gave her long, thin body a waif-like appearance. Terri was in her mid-thirties. Today, she looked much older.

The early morning sun glanced off a crystal that hung in the window and sent splashes of rainbow colors across the table. Even this touch of whimsy failed to lighten the general air of moodiness in the kitchen.

Jane had been almost ready to turn in for the night when Terri had appeared at her door yesterday, overnight bag in hand and all of her earthly possessions crammed in her Toyota. Jane hadn't seen her niece for several years, and almost didn't recognize her as she stood in the light of the porch lamp, shadows falling across her face. She'd only stay for a while, Terri had assured her aunt. She just needed time to sort through things and get her life back on track.

"I wish I could be here with you this morning." Jane glanced at her niece who still hadn't moved from her pensive pose. "But I have to go help Nanette and Marguerite at the Brubaker mansion. We hope to have the tea shop ready by Christmas." Jane wished Terri would nod or give some sign that she had heard her. She folded the dish towel over the drainer and sat down at the table.

"Don't worry about me," said Terri. "I just have a lot to think about. I still have to unpack the car and make a few phone calls. You know, tie up some loose ends."

The whole situation seemed like one big loose end to Jane. "I know this is tough, Terri. It's never easy to lose a job. And to be accused of embezzlement by someone you thought trusted you." Jane shook her head. "You must feel betrayed." She reached across the table to take her niece's hand.

"At least I wasn't officially charged with anything." Terri removed her hand from Jane's clasp and gripped her coffee cup again. "It'll be okay. And, yeah, I can't believe Mrs. Jameson's family would think I could steal from her. I've been her personal assistant for ten years. And besides, her son Tom should know that if I wanted to skim money, I wouldn't leave a paper trail of cash withdrawals. That's almost insulting. I know Mrs. Jameson liked me and I liked her. Her son, though...." Her voice tapered off.

"Well, I know you wouldn't misappropriate funds from your employer. And the son must have known that as well." Jane sipped the last of her lukewarm coffee and took the mug to the sink.

"I might have been framed," continued Terri. "But if I was, it wasn't a professional job. Not like those robberies."

"Wait, what?" Who got robbed?" Jane sat down again. How many more surprises would her niece throw at her?

Terri pushed a lock of untidy hair back from her face and sighed. "There was a rash of break-ins around Northern Virginia, all affluent neighborhoods. Homes of bankers and investment executives. They took money, jewelry and other valuables. Things they could fence and get quick cash for. The Jameson's house was burglarized three weeks ago, and the thieves took some family heirlooms."

Jane's eyes widened. "Good heavens. That's frightening. Yes, my dear. You did the right thing when you moved to quiet Custer's Mill."

Terri's face twisted into a wry smile. "Don't take this the wrong way, Aunt Jane, but I didn't have a slate full of choices. After Tom put old Mrs. Jameson into a nursing home, I was told to leave the place and never show my face there again."

"Well, that was pretty final. Still, I'm glad you're here." Jane said. "I'm sure with your head for business and your finance degree from Georgetown, another job will pop up soon."

Terri didn't answer.

They sat in silence for a few moments until Jane stood. "Tell you what, once you get your things put away and your calls made, come on over to the Brubaker mansion and meet my friends. I know they'd love to see you."

Terri looked doubtful but managed a slight smile. "I'd love to meet your friends, but let me get settled in today. Could I come by tomorrow? I still have a lot of things to sort through."

"Sure, dear, that would be wonderful. Just make yourself at home."

The brass chimes above the door rang a discordant rendition of Big Ben's carillon as Serafina opened the door to the Serendipity Herb shop. Yesterday's post had delivered a large shipment of patchouli leaves, and she breathed in their earthy, musky scent as she walked around the room, opened shades and tied back curtains.

If she closed her eyes at this very moment, the smell could transport her back to another time, to a faraway place. A place where the open road beckoned and walled rooms did not exist. Her longing was real, and the pull strong, but she couldn't go there. Not now. Perhaps not ever. She was a respectable merchant now. A business owner and a responsible citizen of Custer's Mill. Still...

Serafina had opened her shop in July, just in time for the town's 4th of July celebration. For a while she'd wondered if the shop would become a reality. Old Laurence George wasn't the easiest of people to negotiate with. He hadn't trusted her at first. And, truth be told, she couldn't blame him. He'd known her in her wild days. The almost homeless waif who haunted the streets. And then as a teenager. Well, she wouldn't go there at the moment. Suffice it to say, she hadn't done much to inspire trust in the adults of Custer's Mill.

But here she was, and business was growing. The old warehouse wasn't much to look at on the outside, but the location was perfect. She offered a large variety of herbs and spices at rock-bottom prices, and the word soon spread. Even the owners of the bakery in town bought cinnamon and nutmeg from her.

A curtain rustled in the back of the shop, and a black cat half-slinked, half-sauntered into the room, squinting in the bright light that streamed through the front windows.

"Late night, fellow?" The cat raised his nose and then looked away in a haughty gesture that said, "Oh? And what makes you think that my night travels are any of your business?"

She opened a can of tuna and dumped it into a ceramic bowl, and the cat began to devour the fishy flakes.

"Not even a purr to thank me? Ungrateful fur ball." Serafina smiled and placed a bowl of water beside the food.

Midnight had been a foundling of sorts. Although he had been scrawny, dirty, and wild-eyed when he first appeared at the back door of the shop, he'd had a tag around his neck that told the world his name. He was Midnight, and he was a displaced feline. He was used to people. Serafina discovered he was also used to being catered to and adored. She often wondered where he came from and why his owner had disappeared from his life. But he was a good mouser and an excellent listener, so she let him stay in the shop. Besides, what better mascot for an herb shop than a black cat?

"Well kitten, since you are not going to help me package the patchouli leaves, I guess I'll get to work." Midnight ignored her. He was still intent on his tuna feast.

When the clock chimed eleven, Serafina was startled. She hadn't realized she had worked for so long. The fruits of her labors lined the counter. Dozens of plastic bags were filled with patchouli, the tops sealed to keep in the aroma of the pungent herb. She had also attached labels listing a few potpourri recipes. You either loved patchouli or you hated it. There was no middle ground.

Those who loved it always looked for ways to share the scent in the form of potpourri. Those who hated it tended to go for more traditional scents such as lavender and lemon verbena. There were boxes of both herbs in the back. Serafina sighed and wished for the hundredth time that she had a shop assistant.

A sharp meow came from behind her, and Midnight hopped on the counter. With one sweep of his padded paw, he knocked a pile of plastic bags and a basket full of twist ties to the floor.

"Hey. What's the deal?" Serafina cuddled the black ball of fur against her cheek. The cat went limp in her arms and his purr vibrated his entire body. "Feeling neglected? Well, I can relate." She surveyed her empty shop. "I guess we can sit for a minute." She pulled a padded folding chair into a ray of sunlight and closed her eyes.

"Looks like we both found a place to land, huh, kitten?" She stroked the silky fur and rested her head against the back of the chair. "Close your eyes and you can be just about anywhere, kitty." Almost before she realized what had happened, the earthy fragrances in the shop and the warm stream of sunlight worked their ethereal magic. She had resisted the urge to let her imagination roam earlier that day, but this time she seemed to have no choice but to follow its beckoning hand.

Without warning, the walls of the shop melted away, and she was once again in a forested clearing, making camp with the itinerant group of people who had become her temporary family for over three years. She saw it all. The creaking wooden wagons, the cobbled streets of Europe, the dying embers of a campfire. She left them over a year ago, but in some ways, it seemed like yesterday. And in some ways, her gypsy life seemed like it had never happened at all.

When Serafina was a child, she had been fascinated by the stories old Bessie Crawford told her of the nomadic people who used to travel through the Shenandoah Valley selling their wares. These tales painted vivid pictures of a colorful, captivating lifestyle that set Serafina's imagination into ecstasy. Her one dream was to travel with the gypsies. Bessie shook her head and frowned every time Serafina mentioned the idea.

She told Serafina not to waste her time fancying things that would never happen.

But Serafina *had* traveled with the Roma. She spent almost two years on the open road, learned the Romani language, and came to understand the nuances of their culture. She'd created memories that grew more intense as the years passed. She would never forget those warm nights under the stars. There seemed to be more stars in western Europe than anywhere else in the world.

And then there was David. She still remembered the way his dark hair curled around his left ear and hung straight over his right one. But she couldn't think about him now. Not yet. She wondered if the folks in Custer's Mill would believe her stories if she told them. Not that she ever would. This odd and unsettled time of her life held a spot in her heart that was both sacred and terrifying.

Midnight stirred on her lap, dug a sharp claw into her thigh, and brought her back into the present time. "Ouch, you beast." Serafina dumped him onto the floor, and he scampered behind an oriental screen dividing the retail section of the shop from the packing area.

Serafina straightened her skirt and reached her hands to the sky in a full body stretch. She'd continue these ruminations another day. Right now, she had to get back to work.

"Mauve walls. What about two mauve walls and two ivory-colored walls? What do you think, Emma?" Jane stood near the vintage mahogany sideboard, pencil poised in the air. She tried to keep her mind on the tasks at hand and not on the conversation with her niece that morning. Outside, the ancient oak trees were ablaze with color. Fall was in full glory in Custer's Mill. The old Brubaker mansion looked splendid against the harvest gold backdrop of the towering trees. The mountains heralded the onset of autumn with their rustic glow.

"I like it. It's bright, but not too over-the-top." Emma sat in a drop-cloth-covered chair. She watched the ladies bustle about like worker bees on a honeycomb.

"I was thinking more along the lines of forest green," said Nanette as she ran a rough, work-worn finger over the plastered walls.

"Well, I think," said Marguerite, "that we should hire a decorator and not even attempt to do it ourselves. I, for one, have never had an eye for mixing colors."

"I'm not sure we can afford a decorator and make the repairs we need to get this place up and running." Jane put her clipboard on the sideboard and walked toward the window. "Decorators charge a lot of money. Besides we don't want someone to come in and make the place suit their own taste, do we? They wouldn't have known Bertha. I think it's important to keep some of the Brubaker family heritage, you know?"

Nanette sighed. "Jane's right. Besides we already know what needs to be done; we've just got to roll up our sleeves and get busy. So, what's on the list?"

"Well, we need to paint the walls, patch some nail marks in the crown molding, update the plumbing, make or buy new curtains... Shall I continue?" asked Jane.

Nanette nodded. "Sure, why not? I'm already overwhelmed."

"We also need to sort through the upstairs rooms and attic for some smaller tables. This big table was great for a large family, but we'll have to have a more intimate setting for our tea rooms."

"I noticed you said 'rooms.' Do you think we should plan to use both the parlor and the dining room?" asked Marguerite. "The pocket doors will make it easy to close off one room if we have large groups."

"Let's not count our chickens before they hatch," said Nanette. "I think we should start by serving select groups. Maybe plan on tables of four with twelve to sixteen people at a time?"

"And that brings me to a big item on our to-do list." Jane flipped a page on the clipboard. "Installing new kitchen appliances. I don't think we'll bake more than scones and pastries at first, but we might as well get commercial grade appliances. You never know what the future will hold."

"Plus, you have to make sure it fits all building codes for a food establishment," said Emma. "I wonder if Billy can help with that?"

"Don't forget," said Nanette as she ruffled through her overstuffed purse in search of a pen, "Billy's not town manager anymore. He's sporting a reflective vest and picking up trash these days. Community service for sins committed." She pulled a stub of a pencil from her purse and began to scribble on Jane's list. "Still, he might remember the codes and stuff."

They all jumped when the muted tones of the doorbell echoed throughout the house.

"Can you get that, Emma? You can be at the door by the time the rest of us could get out of our chairs."

Emma walked over and pulled the heavy wooden door open.

"How's this for bright and early?" Petey Blue was on the porch. He grinned at her. As usual, his buddy, Marv, stood behind him. Each man carried two buckets filled with odd assortments of painting tools and each clutched a drop cloth under his arm.

"Good morning, gentlemen." Emma motioned for the men to enter. She tried not to wince at the sight of their grimy shoes.

"Well just listen to that Marv. We ain't been bestowed with the title 'gentlemen' for a long time. Maybe we should change our ways and attain to that high calling." Both men began to drop their buckets, brushes, and rollers on to the hallway floor.

"Hey. Watch it. What do you mean, just throwing your stuff on the foyer floor?" Nanette glared at the two men.

"Sorry, ma'am." Petey Blue's grin widened. "We're just itchin' to get started."

"Sorry," said Marv in a quiet voice.

Petey Blue started. "What? Ma'am, you must be some kind of whisperer to get a word out of Marv. I'll bet he hasn't said two words since last Saint Patrick's Day." He pounded his friend on the back.

"You might do well to be more like your friend, here," said Nanette, as she scowled at the man in the paint-stained overalls. "Anyway, we can't seem to decide on the colors we want to use, so just put this stuff on the back porch for now. We don't need to trip over it every time we go outside."

"Yes ma'am. And what would you like us to do in the meantime? Me and Marv came all ready to work. We'd be right disappointed if you sent us home now."

"Do you know anything about plumbing?" Marguerite sounded doubtful.

Petey Blue looked at Marv. "The only thing we do better than painting is plumbing."

"Is that so?" said Nanette.

"True as can be," said Petey Blue. He gave her a solemn wink. "In fact, Marv just got me a twenty-four-inch steel pipe wrench for Christmas last year. It's still in the box."

"Well, let me show you where the leaks are, and you can get your tools out of the truck." Nanette surveyed the paint supplies that littered the floor. "After you put this stuff on the back porch." She left and the two men followed some distance behind her. Jane and Marguerite made their way back to the dining room.

"This furniture is gorgeous." Jane ran her hand over the plastic that covered the wooden pieces. Even through the covers, one could see the richness of the dark mahogany table and the beautiful carvings that enhanced the matching sideboard.

"Miss Bertha would have known how to create an elegant tea shop. No doubt about that." Marguerite pulled back the heavy red velvet draperies and looked out the dining room window into the rose garden. Under the old maple tree, the flowers huddled together as if they sensed their season was about to end. Yet, they still displayed blooms of delicate peach and apricot. "Where do we begin Jane? Nanette's not the only one who feels a bit out of her league."

Jane moved beside her friend. "I still can't believe Bertha left the mansion to us. Think about it. Some of the rooms upstairs haven't been opened in decades."

"I think you're right Marguerite," said Jane. "We don't have the expertise to fix this place on our own."

The two ladies stood in silence. Somewhere in the garden two blue jays squabbled, and the faint voices of Petey Blue and Nanette floated down the long, oak staircase.

The kitchen door slammed. Bertha's long-time gardener, Hiram Steinbacher, stood in the doorway, a pair of pruning shears in his hand.

Although Bertha had bequeathed to Hiram the gardener's cottage on the estate, he still had not told the ladies if he planned to stay on as their gardener. And even though he had become more sociable after his brush with death back in the early summer, he still remained taciturn and almost impossible to read.

"Miss Bertha would've wanted them roses pruned by now." Hiram leaned against the doorway and took care not to enter the room. Like most of Hiram's conversation, this bit of information was not prefaced by a greeting or any of the niceties of usual social interaction.

"Well, Hiram, that's what you need to do then. The roses were Bertha's most prized possessions. We'd like for you to stay on as gardener." Marguerite smiled and Hiram scowled. "Laziness casts one into a deep sleep and an idle person will suffer hunger," was his reply.

"Who's hungry? We don't want anyone to starve around here." Nanette had come back into the dining room just in time to hear Hiram's last words. "Howdy, Hiram. Do those shears in your hand mean you'll stay on as gardener?"

"I'll take care of the roses now." Hiram began to walk away and then turned. "They're Rosemary Harkness roses, you know. Miss Bertha was partial to that color." He didn't leave time for the ladies to comment as he walked back outside through the kitchen door.

"So does that mean he'll stay?" asked Jane.

"He will if he knows what's good for him." Nanette plopped down on a high-backed, Victorian chair. "That cottage is warm and cozy. And Bertha left a special fund to continue his gardener's salary. He'd be crazy to give all of that up to live in his old green van."

"Ladies, Hiram has given me an idea," said Marguerite.

"Oh dear. You going to start communicating in Bible verses too?" Nanette grinned at her friend.

"Very funny. No. What would you say if we painted the walls the color of Bertha's roses. Maybe hues of peach or apricot?"

"Well, I'm not sure about pink walls," Nanette shook her head. "A light shade of green sounds better to me. You know, like the leaves of a rose? Maybe we could hang floral print curtains with pink and peach colors. I think Bertha would approve."

"Sounds like a great idea to me." said Jane. "Shall we check number one off our list? And also, let's all remember to ask our gentlemen painters to be more careful with their muddy boots. There's a pile of dirt in the foyer. Why, they even dragged some in here." She pointed to dark footprints on the wide oak-paneled floor.

She bent to inspect the mud before she scooped it into the dustpan and deposited it in the garbage bin. "Interesting. Usually this area is covered in red clay. But this blue-green color is unusual.

Wonder what minerals are in it? Looks a bit like manganese."

Nanette rolled her eyes. "You science types."

Just then, a sharp bang erupted from overhead. The sound was followed by the steady staccato of hammer blows.

"Good grief. What are they doing up there? Ripping the fixtures from the walls?" Nanette heaved herself from the chair and called from the bottom of the stairs. "Everything okay? Sounds like the apocalypse is upon us."

Incoherent words rumbled under the noise.

"Gracious. I hope they know what they're doing." Marguerite stared at the ceiling.

"I wouldn't bet on it." Nanette scooped her truck keys from the foyer table. "Think I'll go down to the hardware store and check out the options for green paint. She gave her friends a severe look. "I think these next few days could be long ones." Nanette glanced over at Emma who was writing something in her notebook. "Did you take notes on our conversation? Good idea. We can't remember what we say from one minute to the next."

"Just a few observations. Nothing exciting."

Nobody noticed the plastic bag in Emma's hand. She'd salvaged a pile of the blue-green soil from the trash bin.

Nanette backed her Chevy Luv pickup onto the street. Each time the engine turned over in that machine was a miracle as far as she was concerned. Ed at the Custer's Mill service station told her five years ago that her vehicle had about three good months left. She'd managed to stretch those three months out a bit. It wasn't as though she couldn't afford another truck. Money wasn't a problem. She'd just formed an attachment to the aged machine. They'd been through plenty together, and Nanette wasn't quick to relinquish friendships.

She didn't see the man in the neon work vest step in front of her until it was too late to swerve. He'd been in her blind spot and had emerged just as she'd switched into gear to move forward. Fortunately for both of them, she was moving slowly enough for the man to dive out of her way at the last minute. Nanette pounded the brakes and squealed past him.

"What're you doing?" the man screamed. "Trying to kill me?"

"Billy Brubaker?" The fog cleared from her eyes, and Nanette was able to make out the former Custer's Mill town manager. "Didn't you see me backing out? Do you have a death wish, man?" She was angry now. Of all the people to intrude on her peaceful morning.

"I didn't think you'd get into gear that fast." Billy pulled himself from the leaf pile where he'd landed and was brushing bits of dried grass from his clothes. "And I thought you saw me."

"You were doing a lot of thinking, but as usual, in the wrong direction." Nanette shook her head. "Is this where they have you working out your penance now?"

Billy looked at the ground. "Right now, I'm keeping our roads clean and raking leaves on town properties." He looked defensive.

"Serves you right, for letting Pete Anderson bully you all those years."

Billy frowned. "First you try to kill me, and then you insult me. What have I ever done to you?"

Nanette narrowed her eyes and squinted at the chubby, disheveled man. "You know, Billy, that just about sums it up. You haven't done anything to anybody. You're not ambitious enough. You just let people lead you along where they want you to go."

"You're sure talking mean today, Nanette. Nobody here wants to give me a chance. I'm a changed man."

Nanette sighed. "Well, I'm not one to give the benefit of the doubt. I'll keep an eye on you, Brubaker. Maybe you have changed, but you'll have to prove it. Nobody's going to take you at your word again until you've built back trust."

"It's not that easy."

"You're right. It's not easy. But trust takes time. Be patient and just keep on the right side of the law. Keep on the straight and narrow and next year might look a whole lot better. Now, I've got to get going. Got walls to paint."

Petey Blue wiped his mouth with the back of his sleeve. "Whee doggies. Haven't had this kind of grub since our short stint in the U.S. Army, right, Marv? You're a good cook, ma'am."

"I have to admit that I didn't make the cherry tarts and the blueberry scones," Jane said.

"Who did, Jane?" Nanette licked a smear of thick cherry filling from her finger and reached for another pastry.

"They're from the Andes Bakery. They have a new baker. Reba told me he was trained in Paris." Jane broke off a piece of flaky scone. "Just look at that texture."

"Who cares about texture," said Nanette with her mouth full. "Just savor the taste."

"If that were true, dear lady," came a voice from the foyer, "one would relish the taste of chocolate covered cardboard as much as chocolate pie."

"Now, what's he doing here?" Nanette turned toward the door. "Our least favorite bookseller strikes again."

Laurence George came into the kitchen, dropped two boxes on the floor and sat down on top of them. "Hot off the press," he said with a gleam of pride in his eyes. "My first publication, *Custer's Mill. The Little Town with a Big Past.* Just in time for your grand opening." He looked around the cluttered kitchen. "By the looks of things, I'd say they are in plenty of time."

All three women glowered at him. "We're progressing quite well," said Marguerite. "In fact, I would say we are on target for our opening just before Christmas."

"Miracles do happen," said Laurence, "or so they say. Especially at Christmas."

"Ah, yes. Christmas miracles." The ladies hadn't seen Alex George enter behind his brother. It was apparent the two had called some kind of truce.

"He has you working for him now?" said Nanette, eyeing the box Alex was holding.

"Not really." Alex smiled and opened the box. "These are my own estate sale finds. Upscale costume jewelry." He held a green necklace up to the sunshine streaming through the window.

"Why, Alex. That's stunning." Jane rose to examine the piece of jewelry.

"I have several pretty pieces. I was wondering if I could display a few in the foyer of the tea shop. You know, along with my esteemed brother's latest literary masterpiece?"

"I don't think we have a glass case to display them." Marguerite said. "That necklace may well be costume jewelry, but it's nice costume jewelry. I wouldn't feel comfortable just leaving it out in the open."

"I could find a display case if you're okay with me leaving a few pieces here."

The ladies looked at each other and nodded in unison. "I think a few well-chosen pieces of jewelry would add charm to the place," said Marguerite, speaking for the group.

"Well then. It's a deal." Alex turned to help Laurence arrange the boxes of books in the foyer.

Emma glanced at her computer screen. The array of samples looked more like a selection of makeup shades than colors of different soil types. Her amateur vision couldn't discern many of the subtle differences in texture and hue, and her head ached from trying. She rubbed her eyes. Of course, there was no reason to suspect that the soil Jane had found "interesting" had meant anything. In fact, the more she thought about it, the more Emma wondered if she was clutching at straws.

She so wanted to be part of a sleuthing team again. But what kind of investigator invented evidence just so she could feel useful? No doubt she was just being silly. But still, sometimes her hunches were right. She had to believe in herself even if nobody else did.

It was almost closing time. She'd lock the library and mosey on over to the mansion and try to find a natural way to broach the subject of the dirty boots to the two painters. Who knows? Maybe she was on to something.

A few dark clouds hung low over the horizon. The pleasant breezes of early fall had disappeared. Now, dry and falling leaves suggested winter was just around the corner.

Emma found the two vagabond painters behind the house cleaning paintbrushes. Marv was holding the hose as Petey Blue scrubbed the bristles with a wire brush. There appeared to be more paint on the painters than on the brush or in the buckets.

When he saw Emma, Petey Blue stood and bowed. "Well, well. To what do we owe the pleasure? I would shake your hand, but I appear to be a bit smeared in green."

Emma sat down on a stump and opened her notebook.

"Well looky here, Marv. Looks like we're gonna be interviewed. You from the newspaper?" Petey Blue stared at her notebook.

"You know what I do. You've seen me in the library."

"Librarians don't carry notebooks."

"Well, this one does. I have a couple of questions to ask you about the soil around here."

"What?" From the look on his face, it was clear that Petey Blue was not expecting such a question.

"The soil. What kind of dirt do we have around here?"

He scratched a bristly chin. "For starters, look around you. What do you see?" Not waiting for her to answer, he continued, "Limestone and red clay, girl. Limestone and red clay."

Emma nodded. "But to be more specific, that dirt you tracked in on your boots back inside the mansion. Looks peculiar. Not like any kind of soil Jane has seen around here and she's a former earth science teacher."

"Aren't you the detective? What do you think, Marv? Should we put her on our sleuthing team?"

Marv lowered his eyes.

Petey Blue picked up a half-cleaned paint brush and wiped the bristles on the grass, covering the natural green blades with pale emerald paint.

"Well? Where did you get that mud on your boots?" Emma realized her tone was a bit demanding and rephrased her question. "I'm just curious about that unusual soil. I'm a farmer's daughter, you know," she added.

"I'm not rightly sure. Me and Marv go all over creation on our various missions. It could've come from just about anywhere this side of the West Virginny line."

"But where were you recently?" Emma was growing impatient again. Couldn't these yokels just answer a simple question?

"Why, I'd have to consult my diary," said Petey Blue. "And it ain't with me at present. What do you say I take a look tonight and give you a full report tomorrow? He winked at his partner. "Marv and me have to stop by the library anyway. There's a couple more things we need to ask the World Wide Web."

Emma nodded. These men were infuriating, but if she wanted answers, she'd have to play their game. And to be sure, she wanted answers.

Craig MacKenzie, the new baker at Andes Bakery added a drop of vanilla to the batter he was stirring. He was glad he'd convinced the owners that pure oil extracts outclassed their fake counterparts by a mile. Pure extracts were required in Paris where he'd attended culinary school. The frothy mix was beginning to form peaks, and he smiled with satisfaction. Baking was so rewarding and so easy. Put in a few chilled egg whites, a smidgen of cream of tartar, a bit of sugar, and a drop of vanilla; whip the ingredients together. And soon—voilà. Perfect meringues.

When you come to think of it, life itself wasn't that complicated. Put in high quality ingredients, add the right mix of intelligence and street savvy. And voilà—a gratifying existence. Can't forget the intelligence though. He'd seen many a man go down from stupid moves. He for one, was not about to make stupid moves. He enjoyed his life in this town. And he'd seen a few of good-looking women he was interested in getting to know. Especially that gorgeous Serafina Wimsey. That herb shop girl.

Bessie poured warm cola into three glasses and set them on the rough oak table. She'd heard the old pickup coming along the road and knew her unwanted houseguests would be hungry. A pot of black beans had been simmering on the wood stove all day, and she'd sliced the last of the garden tomatoes. A loaf of crusty bread completed the meal. There would be peach cobbler for dessert.

"Smells like home, Marv." Petey Blue opened the screen door and inhaled. "Ah Bessie, you sure know how to warm a man's soul."

"Cut out the sweet talk and just set down."

He and Marv took off their work boots and left them on the front porch. "Ain't got none of them fancy slippers to wear, so I guess you'll have to endure our stocking feet." Petey Blue held his nose and laughed at his own gesture.

Without a word, she motioned for the men to sit around the table.

Petey Blue rubbed his hands together. "Maybe we should ask a blessing on these vittles? You wanna pray, Marv?"

Marv shook his head.

"Alrighty then. We can just thank the Lord ourselves."

The group ate in silence for a while, each savoring the old-fashioned goodness of the simple, hearty food.

With no warning, Bessie spoke. "Revenge is justice." Her voice was tight and raspy.

"Well, sir, that sure came out of the blue, Miss Bessie. Now I'm pretty good at figuring out the female mind and all, but you'll have to enlighten me a bit more as to what you're referring to." Petey Blue shoveled a large spoonful of beans into his mouth and waited.

"Shep's done got what's coming to him. Sweet Glory's name is cleared."

At the mention of the name Glory, Marv grew pale. He pushed his chair back from the table.

"Now just set yourself down, Marv," said Petey. "Ain't nobody gonna say anything bad about your sister. We all know she was a good woman. We all know that Shep went and broke her heart."

Marv scowled, but he sat back down.

"Besides, it was all a long time ago." Petey Blue put his hand on Marv's arm. "Doesn't do nobody any good to harbor hate. It spoils the bones."

"You don't have a sister," said Marv.

For once, Petey Blue had no response. He rubbed his chin and stared at his friend.

"And I don't have a sister, neither, thanks to that no-good murderer," said Marv. He stood again, and this time he didn't return to the table.

Tuesday
October 23

"Anybody home?" the pleasant baritone voice floated down the foyer into the main parlor of the Brubaker mansion.

"I reckon it depends on who's asking." Petey Blue swung one leg over the scaffolding and held a paint bucket over Marguerite's head.

"You're lucky we're not the safety inspectors," said Jake as he and Emma entered the room. "I'd write you up in a heartbeat for that makeshift platform."

"Why, it's as sturdy as a boulder," said Petey Blue as the metal pipes groaned and squeaked with his every move.

"I like that shade of green." Emma said, moving well out of the way of dripping paint brushes. "It's a good mix between sophisticated and cozy."

"Just what we were aiming for. It's called Garden Enchantment." Nanette looked pleased. "What brings you here, Chief Preston? I'd have thought you'd be combing the hills for Shep's hideout."

"We're working on it, ladies." Jake turned over an empty five-gallon bucket and sat down. "The only thing we can do is gather all of the pieces and hope they fit into the same puzzle. I needed a break, so we thought we'd come by and check on your progress."

"It's coming along, as you can see," said Nanette. "Although it's a good thing we've covered the place in drop cloths. Just look at those guys flinging paint." She ducked her head as a slather of paint fell from Marv's brush and landed with a plop an inch from her foot. "See what I mean?"

"They're getting the job done though," said Jake.

"How's it coming along? The investigation, I mean?" Marguerite scooted the step ladder next to Jake and sat down on the bottom rung.

"We're making progress. That's about all I can say for now."

"I love solving puzzles too," said Emma. "Listen to what I've found out about the soil around here. Might be a clue."

"Emma." Jake looked incredulous. "I can't believe you're at it again. This past summer you almost got yourself killed. You're great at deductive reasoning, but we're dealing with a murderer here."

Emma's eyes blazed. "You think I don't know that? If you remember, I was the one who faced a murderer in the last case you worked on. I was the one who figured out the clues well enough to solve the case. I was the one...."

"Emma." Jake cut her off. "That's what I'm talking about. I don't want you in danger any more. I…I mean, we almost lost you once. We don't want to take that chance again."

"Well, in case you haven't noticed, I am capable of taking care of myself. It was no thanks to you that I made it through that tunnel and got away from that killer cop." She closed her notebook and stuffed it back into her purse. "I don't think my presence is needed here anymore. I'm going home."

"Wait, Emma. I'll drive you." Jake fished through his pocket for his keys.

"No thanks. I think I'll walk." The door slammed, and the group inside heard Emma's heels click on the stone path.

"Well, now, this is awkward." Petey Blue scratched his head, leaving his wiry, grey hair sticking up in spikes. "There's no figurin' women. No offense, ladies." He bowed to the group around him. "But you know what? I think it's about quittin' time for all of us. I'd like to get back to the ridge before dark. Okay with you, Marv?"

Marv dropped his roller onto a drop cloth and nodded.

"Well, ladies, I suppose I've done enough damage here for one day. I'm going to head back to the station," Jake said. "I'm sorry about the blow up."

Nanette patted his shoulder. "Now don't you worry a thing about it. Young Emma and Serafina have had a volatile relationship for years. I suspect they'll always rub each other the wrong way. They're oil and water."

Jake looked surprised. "But I didn't mention Serafina."

All three ladies looked at each other. "You didn't need to," said Jane. "Remember, Emma's deductive skills are quite above average."

Jake sighed. "Life would be so much easier if everybody just did what they were supposed to do."

"Yeah," said Nanette, "but then you'd be out of a job."

Jake walked down the steps almost bumping into a thirty-something woman on the path heading toward the mansion. Jake nodded to her. She ignored him and continued on her way.

There was no way to erase the awkward silence that still hung in the air as Terri opened the door. "Hey, Aunt Jane. Thought I'd stop by and see this place you've been talking about. Is this a bad time? I can come back later."

"No dear, we're just about finished for the day." Jane held the door open and ushered her niece into the foyer. "Marguerite, Nanette, this is Terri Allman, my brother's only child."

Marguerite extended her hand to the young woman. "This is a pleasure Terri. We feel like we know you already."

"You might say we've watched you grow up over the years. With all the stories Jane has told us, you're already one of the family." Nanette put her arm around the girl's shoulder.

"Stories?" Terri gave her aunt a quick glance, and shrugged off Nanette's friendly embrace. "What kind of stories?"

"You know, the usual proud aunt stories." Jane said. "I stopped short of pulling out photos every time you sent a new one."

Terri frowned. "Great."

"We understand you are an excellent accountant and a savvy business women with the Jameson Corporation," said Marguerite. "I believe your aunt said you worked with Althea Jameson."

"You've heard of her?" Terri looked uncomfortable.

"Only through your Aunt Jane."

"Yes, I did. Or at least until just recently. Mrs. Jameson was beginning to show evidence of dementia, and her son didn't want her living in that huge house all alone. He placed her in an upscale nursing home, and they didn't need me around anymore."

Jane held her breath, hoping the young woman wouldn't elaborate on the specific circumstances of her former employment.

"That's why she has time to visit with me," said Jane. "We're going to take advantage of Terri's interval between jobs and spend some much-needed aunt/niece time."

"Say, Terri, I have an idea." Nanette's face brightened. "We could use your expertise. Being new business partners, we need some direction in getting our finances for the tea shop in order. Would you be interested in some part-time work while you are here visiting? It wouldn't be as prestigious a job as you are used to, but we could sure use your help. Keep it all in the family so to say?"

"Nanette, that's a wonderful idea," Marguerite paused, trying to gauge how Jane felt about this proposal. "Terri, we don't want to infringe on your time with your aunt. Sorry Jane, if we got too exuberant in our suggestions."

Terri spoke before Jane could respond, "I think this is just what I need. Yes, ladies, I would love to help you get your business organized. Aunt Jane and I will have plenty of time to visit and catch up."

"Super." Nanette said. "Now Terri, come on back to the kitchen with me. There are few of those pastries left and we'll put on the tea kettle. Ladies, you joining us?"

"In a minute," said Jane, twisting a golden fringe on the edge of a dining room curtain.

"Oh, Jane, we did intrude, didn't we?" said Marguerite.

"No, I just think it's been a long day. I have found it very wearing—Petey Blue and Marv's messiness, the spat between Emma and Jake. You know, all of this activity can take its toll on these old bones. You and Nanette have made a gracious offer to Terri. I'm sure it will all work out."

"Of course, it will Jane. Why, you heard Nanette. Terri is family."

Marguerite and Jane headed down the hallway back to the kitchen.

Thursday

October 25

The aroma of fresh roasted coffee and baking bread met Jane and Marguerite at the door of Andes Bakery and Fine Confections.

"Oh, that's just heavenly," said Jane as she folded her umbrella. "Especially in this kind of weather." Outside the wind beat slashes of rain against the windowpanes, and bare branches were tossed about like ghostly arms waving in the dark gray sky.

Marguerite nodded. "Pretty nasty out there. But my, isn't this place delightful. I've already decided I'm taking a loaf of bread and a few of those muffins home with me today." She pointed at the artful arrangement of pastries, breads, scones, muffins, and chocolate candies behind the glass case.

A trim young man in a white apron sprinkled flour on a work table next to a stack of shining stainless steel bowls, and pans of rising dough. The open arrangement of the bakery allowed customers to watch the chefs at work and to see the finished products as they came steaming out of the ovens.

"May I help you ladies?" The man turned and gave the two women a slight bow. His curly black hair flopped across one eye and he tossed his head to avoid using his gloved hands to push it away.

"Well, yes you can," said Jane. "We're here to talk with the owners if they're around. I stopped by a couple days ago, but didn't get your name. I'm Jane Allman and this is my friend, Marguerite White. Your reputation as an outstanding baker is already making its way around town, you know." She smiled.

"My name is Craig MacKenzie. I'm pleased to make your acquaintance,

Ms. Allman. Ms. White. And thank you for your kind words. I've only been here a couple of weeks, so it's nice to know my work is getting off on the right track. I'll ask Minnie to run upstairs and see if Mrs. Andes can come down and chat with you."

A thin middle-aged woman appeared from the back of the bakery. "Sure, I'll go find her, Craig. And can I get you ladies anything?"

"I think we'd both like a cup of coffee, and I'll take one of the black forest pastries," said Jane.

"I'll have my coffee black and one of those blueberry scones." Marguerite settled herself at a table next to the window.

The woman took the desserts from the display case and handed them to the ladies. "Enjoy your pastries and coffees. I'll go see if Mrs. Andes can come down and chat with you. Be back in a jiff."

Half an hour later, the two friends walked out into the chilly morning air. The rain had slackened, but the wind blew from the southwest, scattering dried dead leaves onto the wet pavement and making the sidewalk slippery.

"That couldn't have gone better. Mrs. Andes is on board." Jane pulled up her hood. "Imagine, a baker with Parisian experience to supply our tea shop. We can cross-promote the bakery, plus get a great deal on pastries we serve. Just perfect."

Marguerite held her umbrella high, to avoid poking Jane as they walked. "And I have some wonderful muffins for breakfast in the morning." She held up a white bakery bag with her free hand. "I can't wait to tell Nanette we're about to become a bona fide establishment here in Custer's Mill."

"The place will be bustling soon enough. I've been looking into where and how we need to advertise to attract visitors. Lots to do."

"Hop in, Jane," Marguerite slid into her red Subaru and reached over to unlock the passenger door. "I know you could walk home, but let me drop you off since the weather is so nasty. Save your strength, my dear. We have a lot of work ahead of us."

"Thanks, I believe I'll take you up on that offer," said Jane. "This could be the start of something big for us. And for Custer's Mill. And I say 'bring it on.'"

The women caught a glimpse of the young baker at the window and waved as they pulled away from the curb. Their thoughts were full of excitement about their new venture and the changes it would bring.

Serafina worked throughout the morning, filling muslin bags with dried herbs and restocking shelves. The cinnamon rack was almost empty.

She untwisted the tie of a large plastic bag, and the sweet smell of spices floated into the air. Almost immediately the piquant scent pulled her mind out of the present and plopped her down into, of all places, the Kramer kitchen. Emma's mom had often had a plate of snickerdoodles ready for the girls when they got home from school.

She sighed. Those were good days. It wasn't hard to be Emma's friend then. Now, it was an uphill climb. Serafina wasn't a romantic. She'd accepted the fact that not everybody approved of her free-spirited lifestyle. Thing was, Emma used to be a free spirit too. Oh, she was awkward about it, and you could never get Emma to break rules. But back then, Emma knew how to let go and have fun.

Serafina smiled when she thought about the long, summer days on the Kramer farm. They were magic. Those were the days she missed. That was the Emma she missed.

Mrs. Kramer had called both Serafina and Emma "her girls". Serafina never remembered her own mother baking after-school treats. In fact, she was not often at home when Serafina got off the bus.

Emma's perfect life had ended in college when Eric died. Then soon after that, cancer took her mom. In some perverse way, Serafina had found satisfaction in Emma's losses. But she knew they were her losses too. Especially Mrs. Kramer.

A loud pounding on the back door of the shop brought her back to the present. Midnight jumped from the window sill and ran behind the curtain. Serafina couldn't imagine who'd be using the back entrance. She wasn't expecting any deliveries until later in the day. She slid the lock and opened the door. Alex George stood on the stoop, his fist raised ready to knock again.

"Well, you're making an unnecessary racket. Come on in, the door is open."

Alex bowed. "Please forgive my rudeness. I beg your pardon." He edged past her into the shop. "Mmmmm. Do I smell cinnamon?"

Serafina was annoyed. Her morning had been going so well, and now this intrusion. "What do you need, Alex?"

"Well, I believe it's customary for neighbors to visit each other, don't you think? I've been moving my things into the warehouse for several weeks—I'd have thought you'd be over to see me again." He pursed his mouth into a petulant moue.

"Sure, I heard you banging around over there. I also heard rumors that you've taken over the Bard's Nest. I can't believe Laurence would let you push him around since you just up and disappeared after your dad died. Left him to take care of everything."

"You haven't changed I see. Still the same spitfire." He walked over to the row of shelves on the wall. "Nice shelves." He rubbed his hand along the rough wood. "Walnut is so hard to find these days. Hand-hewn, aren't they?"

"Shep made them for me." She wasn't sure why she had given away that bit of information.

"Ah, the dear, departed Shep. When did you and Shep become an item?" He appeared genuinely curious. "You two were close, were you?"

"Seriously? Shep was old enough to be my grandpa. We were never an 'item', but we were friends. He helped me out over the years. When I started my own business, Shep and his grandmother, Bessie, were there for me." She sealed a bag of cinnamon and placed it in the box under the shelves. "Bessie has always been like family to me. She taught me most of what I know about herbs."

"Then I guess Shep's death has been hard for you," said Alex. He followed her as she moved around the shop. "Who do you have to help you now, Serafina?" he said, his voice soft and full of meaning.

She backed away. "I take care of myself, Alex. I don't need anyone." He was making her uncomfortable, and she wished he would leave.

"I remember you as a waif of a girl who always seemed to be out wandering the woods. Weren't you and Emma Kramer best buddies back then? It seems I always saw you together."

"I could ask what you were doing, stalking little girls. How'd you know so much about me?" She moved to the back of the room and opened the door to the warehouse hoping this would give him a hint. "I'm sure you have other things to do besides spend time with me."

Alex ignored her comment about his knowledge of her past. "Well, like I said. I wanted to be neighborly and say hello. We may need to help each other out from time to time—just like Shep helped you. I wouldn't want you to think that you were all alone."

"I've got work do. So. If you don't mind leaving now." Serafina turned back to the counter and began filling bags with cinnamon sticks.

"Sure, I'll go," said Alex. "But one more thing. You didn't help hide Shep these past few months, did you?" Alex stepped close to Serafina and held her by the arm in a firm grip. He pulled her around to face him. "I've heard that he might have hidden in those old caves. I wouldn't want you in trouble with the police. Shep never was any good. Always involved in some shady deal. And then that mess with Emma. Might not be too good for you if people start connecting the two of you."

Serafina jerked her arm free. "What concern is that to you? Don't worry about me." She gestured emphatically toward the door. Alex gave her a chilly smile, then turned and left the shop. But his last words hung in the air. Serafina drew in her breath. She closed the door with a bang and locked the deadbolt.

Midnight slinked out from under the curtain.

"I don't blame you, boy. He's an oily one. Let's hope we don't have any more unexpected visits."

Though it was early evening, Jake Preston was still at his desk. He tapped his foot against the linoleum floor. Nothing made him more restless than waiting. Justice Atkins had called him a half hour ago with an overview of the autopsy results. He promised a full report by fax within the hour.

As if on cue, the machine beeped. The report had arrived. Jake walked through the dusky office to retrieve the papers. Back at his desk, he pulled a yellow highlighter out of the drawer and settled in to read.

Atkins did good work. And on a case like Shep Crawford's, the answers Jake got from the medical examiner would further direct his investigation.

The samples from the cave matched Shep's blood. Shep was dead when he went in the river. No water in the lungs. There was a blunt injury to his skull. Time of death was probably early morning October twelvth. His killer or killers tried to sink the body to the bottom of the river where it wouldn't be found for months. Which would have worked if it hadn't been for Noah Lambert and his fishing pole.

Noah Lambert. Jake made a mental note to send Jason Dove out to talk the boy again. He was certain Noah was holding something back when he'd questioned him. Dove was Noah's assistant soccer coach. He'd know if Noah was acting strange.

Jake turned his attention back to the report, swiping the yellow highlighter over details for further investigation.

Fishing for clues. Fishing for the truth.

Saturday

October 27

Frost hovered in the air. The woods along the river were carpeted with fallen leaves. "Breathe in that fresh air, boy. Nothing like the beauty of God's green earth to wipe away life's worries." Hiram's voice broke a long silence. For the past ten minutes, he and his companion had trudged along the path without speaking.

The pair carried fishing tackle and ambitious-looking stringers. They'd have to decrease the marine population of the river by a fair amount to fill that chain.

Hiram glanced over at his grandson. Young Noah wasn't acting right. In fact, he hadn't acted right since the day he'd found Shep Crawford's body floating in the river. Couldn't blame the kid, though. Seeing a dead body when you'd been expecting a quiet fishing trip would be enough to mess with anybody's head. Time spent outside in the fresh air would do the child good.

He'd had trouble getting Noah to agree to the fishing trip. That was noteworthy in itself. Usually the boy was chomping at the bit to go fishing. Hiram thanked the Lord that Noah wasn't addicted to that devil box that seemed to be blaring nonstop in his daughter

Sissy's house. He hadn't raised her that way. But to be fair, it was that husband of hers who was glued to the T.V. Sissy never seemed to have enough time to sit down.

"Down at the gas station, they said they're bitin' on worms now. Did you bring enough?"

Noah nodded. "Not many worms at the house this time of year. I dug some in the garden and found about half a dozen. Mom took me to the gas station and we bought a plastic tub full. Should be enough." Noah held a canvas bag in one hand and the lead of his dog, Lightning, in the other. Lightning didn't seem to understand why he was being held back when there were so many fascinating smells in the air and places to explore.

"I expect you can let the dog run now. We're far enough away from the road."

"Yeah, I know." said Noah, still holding the leash. "I just like him to walk beside me; that's all."

Hiram felt a pang of sadness. It's one thing to have the darker side of life rob your freedom. It's another thing to stand by and watch it rob those closest to you. He knew Noah would encounter other tragedies in his lifetime. It was just the way it was. Life threw curveballs. He prayed the kid would have the strength to endure the things he'd have to face.

"Papaw? Do you think God punishes people right away, or do you think he waits a while?"

Hiram glanced at his grandson. "What do you mean, boy? The Bible says that God is slow to anger. What're you getting at?"

Noah stopped to pull a burr from his pant leg. "Well, Daddy said that Shep was a bad man, and he blamed you for something you never did. Do you think God waited 'til now to punish him? Do you think Shep died because he was mean a long time ago?"

Hiram wiped a hand over his bristled chin and looked off into the distance. A vee of geese was headed south, all flying in perfect formation except for one that lagged behind. Hiram had always identified with the ones who lagged, the slow, and the off-kilter. He'd felt that way most of his life. He'd tried to put that mess with Shep and Pete out of his mind. It had all happened years ago, but it had impacted his life ever since. And now, here it was again, rearing its ugly head. And this time by his grandson.

"One thing I've learned, boy, is not to second guess God. He has his reasons for what he does, and his reasons are perfect. Whether or not we understand them. Know what I mean?"

Noah nodded. "I think so. Some people say you're crazy because you quote the Bible all the time."

Hiram let a tiny smile escape from his thin lips. "Do they now? Well, I reckon what I say does sound like foolishness to most people. But those words from the good book find their way into my mind about every time I need to say something."

"Wish I always knew what to say."

"Well, boy, I don't know as I can teach you something like that. Let me ponder on it. But now, why don't you pick out your fattest night crawler and hook him up? I think there's some hungry fish in that river."

"I kinda feel bad killing a worm to catch a fish," said Noah. "But nothing else seems to work."

"Folks have been fishin' in this river a lot of years. Fish got spoiled on worms long time ago. You know, when there wasn't any other kind of artificial bait. They're used to the real thing."

The fishermen threw their lines into the water and watched the red and white sinkers bob on the surface. Noah had released the dog, and his excited yips echoed in the woods as he first treed a squirrel and then chased a rabbit back into its hole.

"Yessiree, this place has a lot of history." Hiram leaned back and rested his pole between his knees. "Heard once that George Washington named the place. Called it Shenandoah after some Indian warrior. Also heard it was named after the Senendo tribe. Who knows?"

"What about Civil War times? Did the armies fight here?"

Hiram scratched his head. "I don't rightly recall a lot of the stuff I learned in history class. I know Sheridan marched through the Valley and burned a lot of homes and farms. And I know old Stonewall Jackson led a campaign here. You like history, boy?"

Noah reeled in his line. "Think some fish just got my worm for breakfast." He strung on another worm before he answered his grandfather. "I got something to show you, Papaw."

Hiram nodded his head, not commenting on the fact that Noah hadn't answered his question.

With one hand, Noah reached into his pocket and pulled out a wrinkled plastic bag. He handed it to Hiram, and then turned his gaze back toward the river. "I wrapped it up in plastic to protect it."

Hiram shook his head and examined the silver coin Noah had handed him.

"Well?" Noah leaned so close his head was touching Hiram's. "What do you think? Nate's dad found some old Civil War stuff in their backyard when they dug their garden."

Hiram fingered the coin through the plastic, whistling through his teeth. "Looks like it's from the Civil War time. Look. I can just make out that date. 1861."

Noah's eyes widened. "You think it's worth a lot?"

"There's no way for me to know. Why don't you take it down to the library and get that Kramer girl to take a look at it? She might be able to find out something about it."

"Been wanting to do that." said Noah. "She helped me find stuff out about steam engines for my history report. Got an A on it."

"Exactly where'd you find the coin?"

Some of the sparkle left Noah's eyes and he became interested in a shoelace that had become untied.

"Boy, I asked you a question."

"Right around that bend." He pointed north. "I found it here. You know, the day I saw the… the day I saw the man."

"You found it here, by the river?"

Noah nodded.

"Well, in that case, I'd be mighty careful who I showed it to."

"You mean I shouldn't show it to Miss Emma?"

"Now don't go puttin' words in my mouth." He handed the coin back to Noah. "I didn't say that. I think you could show her. She could help you out. Just don't go broadcasting it all over town. Understand?"

Suddenly, Noah's pole jumped. "I got a fish!" he yelled.

"Reel him in. Reel him in." It did Hiram's heart good to see joy settle over the boy's face.

"Wow! It's a native trout. They're hard to catch, aren't they?"

"They're sneaky, for sure," agreed Hiram as he helped unhook the squirming fish and secure him on the chain. "We'll have supper tonight."

"Now it's your turn, Papaw."

Hiram leaned back and turned his face toward the sunlight streaming between two old pine trees. He was glad for these rare moments of pure peacefulness, even though they were often sprinkled with times of heavy sorrow. For a long time, he'd waited for life to settle down. To smooth out into routine days of tending the garden, fishing, and relaxing under the sweeping maple tree in the Brubaker yard.

But those days never seemed to come. Since Miss Bertha's death, things had turned even more perplexing. There was something going on now. Something he couldn't quite put a finger on. Something mighty uncanny. Miss Bertha was murdered, and now this thing with Shep.

"Got another one already." The excited voice of his grandson brought Hiram back to the present.

"You're just the better fisherman, boy."

Noah grinned. "Mama's gonna be happy."

Sunday

October 28

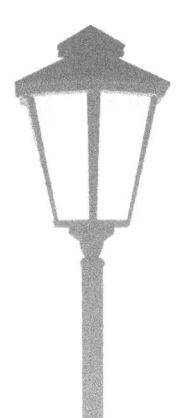

"Thanks, Aunt Jane. I do appreciate you taking me in. I know I sometimes come across as less than grateful, but I don't know what I would have done if you hadn't let me stay here." Terri speared the last piece of chicken on her plate and smiled at her aunt. "You have a group of unusual friends, too. But I like them. At least they seem sincere. Sort of 'what you see is what you get.'"

Jane nodded. "True statement. And their job offer was generous, don't you think?"

Terri narrowed her eyes. "Ye-e-e-es. I believe so."

"We're still figuring out the ropes. We haven't gotten used to owning Bertha's mansion yet, let alone being business partners." Jane shifted in her chair. "I know that your expertise in accounting and money management will be a great help to us." She hesitated. "I just want to make sure you realize these ladies are my dearest friends...."

"Really? I think you can cut the explanation right there. I get it. You don't want me to screw up or take advantage of your friends." Her face was defiant. "I thought you believed me. That you knew none of the allegations Tom made were true. I'm not a thief." Terri stood up, but Jane put a gentle hand on her arm and she sat back down.

"I'm sorry. That's not what I meant," Jane seemed at a loss for words. "It's just, well, with your parents out of the country, I feel responsible…" Her voice trailed off.

Terri shook her head. "I don't believe this. Aunt Jane, I'm thirty-three years old. I don't want or need a nanny. I'd appreciate it if you'd just trust me. I'm not going to mess with your friends."

"I do trust you, Terri. And thank you. Thanks for being willing to help us out."

Terri nodded. "Again, I don't mean to sound like an ungrateful slob. I just get so irritated at having to prove myself over and over."

"I understand," Jane folded her napkin and placed it beside her plate.

"And thank you for dinner. I hate to eat and run, but I have to get more of my things unpacked. I'm meeting Nanette at the mansion at 8:30 in the morning. We're going to the bank to open a new account for the tea shop."

"Don't you let Nanette boss you around," Jane said. "Just remember, you're the expert."

Jane watched her niece climb the stairs. She hadn't said all she wanted to say, but she was sure she'd cut the conversation where it needed to end. She would have to trust Terri. Assume she was being honest. Unless…

By the time Terri reached the top of the stairs, she felt like the wind had been knocked out of her. Her anger had been replaced with a nagging feeling of defeat. Did everyone think she was a thief? If her own aunt didn't believe her, what chance did she have with strangers?

There were two guest rooms in the cozy Cape Cod. Terri had chosen the largest. She opened the door and heaved a sigh. This room looks like my life. A mess. Boxes of various sizes were stacked on the floor around the room, and her bed was piled with an assortment of luggage.

She flipped the rusted clasps of the largest leather bag and peered inside. She was looking forward to unpacking her clothes. In the past, she'd always dressed in the latest professional styles and colors. She knew she was attractive and she chose clothes to accentuate her best features—a small waist and long legs.

Coordinating her closet by the colors of her suits and dress slacks brought order to her life—beige, gray, navy, black. Terri fingered the edge of a pale blue silk blouse. Just feeling the richness of the fabric brought her some solace. 'Dress for success' her professors at Georgetown had told her. As an accountant, she was stepping into a man's world. She needed to look the part. Intelligent. Confident. Successful.

And she had been successful. She'd untangled number mazes like they were so many knotted chains. But ten years of achievement had vanished with one accusation. All of her accomplishments down the drain with a single allegation. Terri wondered if she would ever feel self-assured again.

As she finished pulling out the last pair of slacks, she smiled. Ah yes. How could she have forgotten? At the bottom of the case lay a different sort of proof of her success. A pair of ornate candlesticks and a flat jewelry box.

She held the candlesticks and wiped away a smear. She placed them on the edge of the dresser and watched the polished brass sparkle in the glow of the lamplight. An image of elegance. Of wealth. Of power.

She turned her attention to the box and opened it with care, lifting the contents one by one. A pearl necklace. A gold chain with a large topaz stone. But they didn't hold a candle to her most cherished possession. They paled in comparison to her real treasure.

Reaching to the bottom of the box, she removed a dazzling diamond cocktail ring and held it to the light. The beam from the lamp caught each facet of the stunning jewels, sending rainbows of colors bouncing off the bedroom walls. "Yes." she whispered. "For all your hard work and dedication, you deserve this.

Monday

October 29

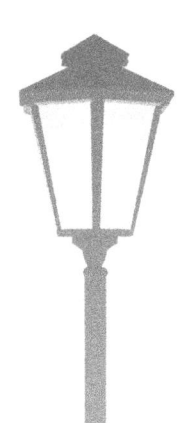

"Man, this old truck's never gonna be the same." Petey Blue surveyed the rusty vehicle and shook his head. "We shouldn't have run her on those steep grades, but there was no other way to get there."

Marv nodded. "Pretty much tore off the fender when we hit that washed-out place."

Petey Blue sighed. "Just part of the trials and tribulations you go through when you're treasure hunters. Especially when you're after a couple of different kinds of treasures."

"Always varmints hanging around treasure." Marv kicked a tire and Petey Blue drew back in alarm.

"Hey, watch it. I just put those tires on a couple of months ago. Considering our financial situation at the moment, these babies need to last a long time."

Marv looked embarrassed. "Sorry. I just get so worked up over the meanness in people."

"You and me both, Marv." Petey Blue shook his head. "Sometimes makes a person wonder why the good Lord just doesn't send a flood and start it all over again." He pulled down the tailgate and propped a foot on the crumbling metal. "But then, I reckon he promised he wouldn't do that again." He glanced at the bed of the truck and brightened. "At least we got the saplings. They ought to be easier to keep an eye on up at Bessie's house."

"Until they find out they're missing from the test farm."

"You're just one big bundle of joy today, Marv. There's no earthly reason why the average citizen shouldn't be allowed plant these trees."

"You know what the man said. Those trees were for authorized testers only. Not for common folk like you and me."

"That's crazy. Nobody owns nature."

"Yep. But they owned that piece of land we took the trees from." Marv shook his head. "They'll miss those saplings soon enough."

"Now don't you go worrying your head about it, Marv. From the looks of that place, nobody goes there much at all. And what's a few trees? You think they're gonna notice?"

"Sins always catch you." Marv shook his head. "You think you're being sneaky. Think nobody sees or hears you. Then bam." He struck his fist into his open palm. "You get caught. Quick as a mouse in a trap."

Petey Blue jumped. "You scare the livin' daylights out of me, Marv. I'm pretty jittery these days. And I'll tell you, it's not because of a couple of American chestnut test trees."

Marv nodded. "I reckon I know what you mean."

"You know, Nanette was right. Light green is the perfect color for these walls. The room feels a lot more customer-friendly." Marguerite stood in the archway between the dining room and the parlor surveying the tea room renovations. "The color pulls the garden into the room. And the tables are angled just right so guests will get a wonderful view of Bertha's roses."

She pointed to several tables of various shapes placed in both the parlor and dining room. The white linen cloths draped at each corner contrasted with the dark wood of the curved Georgian table legs. Shafts of sunlight streamed through the tall windows washing the dining room in a soft glow.

"Now that the downstairs is painted, we can finally see this place beginning to take shape," said Jane. "Amazing. All these tables were hidden away in the attic. And the trunks full of table linens were a real find. Bertha's family must have done some serious entertaining in their day."

Nanette emerged from the kitchen with a large glass vase of peach-colored roses. "Hiram brought these into the kitchen just a minute ago. The last of Bertha's Rosemary Harkness roses for this season. It seems fitting they should have a place of honor." Nanette placed them on the sideboard.

"I think we should keep fresh-cut flowers on the tables as often as we can," said Marguerite. "That would be a nice touch and add a bit of Bertha's personality in each room, every day."

The ladies stood for a few minutes, admiring the beauty around them. They could almost see their old friend nodding her head in approval.

"By the way, folks, guess what?" Nanette paused to make sure the others were listening. "I believe Hiram is staying in the cottage. I got here earlier than usual this morning and noticed the lights on in his kitchen. Hiram was standing by the stove flipping pancakes. Looks like he's settling in. Guess we'll have to get used to seeing that abominable green van parked over there."

"At least he's not still living in it," said Marguerite. "Wonder why he didn't come out and tell us he decided to stay?"

"I think we know there's no rhyme or reason to what Hiram does. And even if there is, who could understand it?" said Nanette.

"Well, I don't think he's adjusted to all of us being here in Bertha's house and in charge," said Jane. "He's taken care of the gardens and watched over Bertha for more than twenty years. We know how much we miss Bertha. I think Hiram misses her a lot more."

Nanette nodded, "Yes, and we're making changes. Never a good thing in Hiram's eyes. Let's just hope he can handle having people come and go when our tea room is opened."

"Well, at least he seems to be tolerating Marv and Petey Blue." Jane checked her watch. "Did you know that they've almost finished putting in the new toilets and fixing the leaks in both of the bathrooms? They've earned their money in my book. Even the old tile floors look brand new."

"They suggested we think about adding showers. Those old tubs are romantic, but not too practical." said Nanette. "Especially if we decide to the rent the rooms out. Not something we have to do right now. Who knows what costs we have ahead of us with this venture?"

"Speaking of Marv and Petey Blue, they've told me they're taking the afternoon off," Marguerite said. "Something about some research for a project they're working on. Not sure what that's about."

"Well, Marguerite, you and I are on duty at the library this morning," Jane checked her watch once more. "It's about time for us to get going. Will you be all right here while we're gone, Nanette?"

"Sure, why wouldn't I be? Besides, Terri will be here in a few minutes. We have a lot of financial stuff to go over." Nanette hesitated. "I do think you should check on Emma though. See how you think she's doing. Whatever this dust-up is between her and Serafina, it's getting pretty nasty."

"I agree," said Jane. "But I think it's more than just jealousy. It goes back to what happened when they were in college, you know, with Eric's death and Emma's need to return to Custer's Mill for those last few months before her mother passed away. So tragic. I wonder if Emma is still working through it."

"Sometimes it seems Emma is stuck in the past. Like time hasn't done its healing work. I'm concerned about the girl."

"We're all concerned about her," said Jane. "That's why it's important we make sure we don't shirk our duties at the library. We need to keep Emma and the library's needs in mind as we move forward with our own plans. Emma is family, and you don't neglect family when they're hurting."

"You know how to run this thing, Marv?" Petey Blue pushed his chair back from the flat screen in front of him. "I got it turned on, I think. What do we do from here?"

Marv stuck his tongue out of the corner of his mouth and stared at the computer monitor. "Maybe we need some help."

"Truer words were never spoken." Petey Blue scratched his grizzled chin. "I saw Miss Marguerite and Miss Jane come in the back door. They can get us connected to the World Wide Web." Petey

Blue tipped back his chair and raised his hand as if he were schoolboy and the library the classroom. "Couple of old geezers over here need some tech-no-logical help."

Jane left her half-full cart and walked over to the two men. "Good afternoon gentlemen. What's up?"

"Well, I see a green light, so I think the power is connected. I'm not sure what to do next." Petey Blue allowed his chair to settle all four legs back on the floor. "Me and Marv have some researching to do, and we would like to connect to the Web to see what we can find."

"Easy enough." Jane made a couple of clicks on the computer. "Okay, you're good to go. Just type in your question or any information you want to find and click 'search.'"

"That's it?" Petey Blue said. "I think I can handle that. Much obliged for your help." He pulled a shaft of papers from a worn knapsack. "We should be good to go."

"Let me know if you need anything. I'll just be over here shelving books."

"Will do." said Petey Blue as he used his index finger to type the letters *a-m-e-r-i-c-a-n-c-h-e-s-t-n-u-t*.

"Miss Emma?"

Emma was glad for an interruption from the quarterly budget she was attempting to decipher. A freckled-face boy stood in front of her.

"Why, Noah. What brings you here? Want to sign up for our fall reading program?"

Noah Lambert looked down at his worn tennis shoes. "Nah, Miss Emma. I get enough reading in school. I don't figure I need to read evenings and weekends too."

Emma smiled. "Well then. What can I do for you?"

Noah shifted from one foot to the other, his fingers curled around a small plastic bag. "I was wondering if maybe you could help me check something?"

"Sure. I might need more information though."

Noah grinned and plopped the plastic bag on the counter. "It's about this. I need to know what it is, and if it's worth anything."

Emma stared at the coin inside the bag. "Oh my. That's amazing. Where did you find such a treasure?"

"Do you think it's worth some money?" Noah's voice rose half an octave.

"We'll have to see if we can find it in our coin reference books. And you still didn't answer me. Where did you get it?"

"Found it," he mumbled.

Looking at the tight line of Noah's mouth, Emma knew that she would have to be content with that answer. For now.

"May I hold it?"

Noah dropped the bag in her hand. She peered through the plastic wrap. "Looks like the date is 1861." She could just make out the words 'Confederate States of America' and 'Half-Dollar'.

"What do you say we look it up online?"

Noah nodded and held out his hand. "Maybe I'd better carry it," he said. "It might be fragile."

"Sure thing, Noah. It's your treasure."

They walked to the kiosk of computers. Aside from Petey Blue and Marv on the corner monitor, and Laurence George in the back, there was no one else at the computer table.

"Let's Google 'Confederate States of America coins.'" Emma punched in the information and was rewarded by a long list of websites. She clicked on the first link. And there it was. An 1861 Confederate States of America half-dollar.

Noah leaned over Emma's shoulder, and both of them saw it at the same time. The estimated value of the coin was $3,000 to $10,000. If it's genuine.

"Wowzers. That's a lot of green-backs," said Emma. Emma and Noah both looked up to see Petey Blue and Marv looking at the computer screen. "Where'd you find that coin, boy?"

Noah's face reddened, and he put the bag back in his pocket. "Ain't nothing," he mumbled.

Petey Blue whistled. "You must have an awful lot of money to turn up your nose at three thousand dollars. But there's fakes out there. Might not be not real anyway."

Noah's face fell.

"Where'd you find it, my lad?" Petey Blue moved closer to Noah, and Noah stepped back. "Nowhere. Just while I was fishing."

Petey Blue's face brightened. "You like to fish, do ya? That's a dying art—fishing is. Boys these days would rather sit in front of a video game screen and play Atari all day."

"Play *what*?"

"Atari was popular several decades ago," said Emma. "I doubt Noah has ever heard of that gaming system. And, sir, it's considered impolite to watch what others are doing on computers. I'm sure you wouldn't want that to happen to you." The obvious greed in the mountain man's eyes made her feel protective of Noah.

"My apologies, ma'am. Young sir. Still learning the ropes about the Web, you know."

A library patron approached Emma. Though she was reluctant to leave Noah with the older man, she was required elsewhere. "Let me know if you need any more help, Noah. You take care." She looked sternly at Petey Blue as she turned to leave.

Ignoring Emma's gaze, Petey Blue pulled up a chair and sat near Noah. "Know anything about trees, boy?"

Noah shook his head. "Not much. We have a couple of maple trees in our backyard. Branches are low. Good for climbing."

"Well, if you ever aim to learn anything about dendrology, just call me."

"Den-*what*?" Noah looked confused. "Is that a video game too?"

Petey Blue laughed. "A video game? What do they teach you youngins in school these days? Dendrology, my boy, is the study of trees. Plain and simple."

"Well the word isn't so plain and simple. It has four syllables."

"Four *what*?" Petey Blue leaned his head toward Noah.

"Syllables. You learn about syllables in school, you know." Noah clapped out the parts of the word.

"Well I'll be," said Petey Blue. "I reckon they do teach a few things now and again."

Back at the front desk, Emma found the page she and Noah had been looking at. Before moving away to check out a small girl's books, she sent it to the printer in her office. The coin and the old man had her curious. And a bit disturbed.

Tuesday

October 30

The kitchen at the Preston house was littered with paint tubes, fabric scraps, cardboard boxes, and crayons. Jake surveyed the mess, and beyond it all, saw the composed, immaculately dressed form of his young daughter.

"Why, who is this gorgeous princess emerging from the rubble?" Jake started to pat the strawberry blond ponytail and then thought better of it when he saw Kate frown.

"I'm Violet Baudelaire. You know, the oldest girl in The Series of Unfortunate Events? Dad. Come on. You've read Lemony Snickett stories enough. You should know."

So he was 'Dad' again. He looked at his daughter swathed in cascading black ruffles and sighed. There was no doubt about it. Kate was growing up.

"Oh yeah. I see it. The dress. The boots. Makes perfect sense now."

Kate rolled her eyes. "Hurry. We're supposed to meet Noah and Missy at 4:00. Do you have my pumpkin candy basket?"

"Right here, ma'am." Jake gave his daughter a sweeping bow and opened the door with a flourish. "After you."

When Jake and Kate arrived, downtown Custer's Mill was already teeming with ghouls, goblins, superheroes, and book characters. Main Street had been turned into a pedestrian walkway, and food vendors lined the sidewalks.

"There's Noah, Dad." She waved and spun around to show off her costume. "I'll walk around with him. And maybe Missy, if we can find her." Kate was off before Jake could give her his usual parental warning to be careful.

"Good looking costume, there, Chief Preston." He hadn't heard Serafina come up behind him. She looped her arm through his. "Dressed like a regular guy, I see. But I'd know that handsome face anywhere."

Jake unlinked his arm from hers. "Kate's hoping to fill her candy basket to the brim with sweets this evening. I feel sorry for her teacher tomorrow."

"She should be able to do that in fifteen minutes. Did you see all of those vendors giving away candy? Let's go over and get a doughnut from the Andes Bakery. Talk about melt-in-your-mouth." She grabbed Jake's arm again and tugged him toward a blue canopy on the corner.

Although the Halloween event had just started, there was already a long line of people in front of the Andes Bakery tent. The staff from the bakery appeared to be making doughnuts to order, on the spot. The sweet smell of deep-fried sugar filled the air, sending a tantalizing signal to Jake's nose.

"There's a long line here. Maybe we should come back later."

"It's only going to get longer," said Serafina, planting her feet and refusing to budge for a young child trying to make his way closer to the front of the line.

"She's right, you know." The voice came from behind and Jake turned to greet Albert Nelson and his lady friend, Mia Kramer.

"Why, Professor Nelson. Mia. I haven't seen you two for weeks it seems. How are you?"

Professor Nelson smiled and spun his cane in a jaunty motion. "Better than I have been in years. This young lady keeps me on my toes, and it's good for an old man to keep dancing." His eyes twinkled as he looked down at Mia, who smiled back.

"Now Albert, you know as well as I do that your energy level surpasses mine any day." Mia turned to Jake. "So how do you like patrolling a small town? The job must be much less exciting than your position as a county detective."

Jake smiled. "I've got plenty of excitement at the moment. And being Kate's dad provides its own thrills these days."

"I'll bet. Emma says she is turning into quite the entomologist."

"Yeah, I'm not sure what she will do when the frost sends the bugs scurrying for shelter. I guess she'll just go on a quest to find insects that can survive winter temperatures." Jake felt uneasy at the mention of Emma's name. He had no idea where he stood with her at the moment. And now, here was Serafina trying to hang onto him.

"My dear, I think we should check out the musical ensemble under the gazebo. Perhaps the line for doughnuts will shrink after a while."

"And I'm sure those pastries will be worth the wait, Albert. Is that a steel guitar I hear?"

"I love that sound," said Serafina. "Makes me think of exotic beaches. Or late night campfires." Her voice trailed, and she seemed to disappear down a long forgotten path. A path no one in Custer's Mill could imagine. Or follow. Suddenly, she stepped away from Jake and turned toward the older couple. "Mind if I tag along with you two?"

"Not at all," Mia answered.

"But that doesn't mean I've forgotten about those doughnuts." Serafina smiled up at Jake. "I'm expecting a gooey, glazed one when I get back."

The trio waved goodbye to Jake and walked toward the soulful music coming from the center of the lawn.

The bakery's menu was simple, and for that, Jake was grateful. He didn't want to face the decision of choosing from fifteen different kinds of doughnuts. Glazed or unglazed. Those were the selections.

The young man taking the orders looked slightly familiar to Jake.

"Hi there, officer." he said.

Jake returned the man's smile. "Man, I can't even dress in plain clothes anymore without everybody recognizing me." Jake wondered how such recognition might be affecting his work on Shep's murder.

"You just have the 'look' I guess. Plus, you know this is a small town. So. What can I get for you? Sir?" The young man was staring at him. "Glazed or unglazed?"

Jake started. "Oh, two glazed, please. Why not? And a cup of your dark roast coffee."

The man handed Jake his change. "By the way, I'm Craig MacKenzie. New chef at Andes Bakery. Nice to meet you."

He picked up a doughnut with piece of waxed paper and passed it to Jake. "This one's still warm. Enjoy."

Jake thanked him and carried his coffee and donuts to a vacant bench nearby. The evening was unseasonably warm, and not a breeze stirred. Amidst the laughter and flurry of activity, he felt a sudden calm. A peace he hadn't felt since…since before Mirabelle's death. He wanted to cling to the moment.

Jake caught a glimpse of Kate talking to Sissy Lambert's boy, Noah. Custer's Mill was a good place for Kate. For both of them. He closed his eyes, and took a big bite of the warm, doughy treat. If Serafina didn't hurry back, he might eat the other one too.

"That was totally the most fun I've had ever! I can't wait 'til next Halloween. Next year I'm going as an elf princess. Nanette can help me make my costume. It'll be the coolest one here." Kate had been talking nonstop since they'd left the festivities, and Jake was only half-listening to the chatter.

"And Noah told me it's a secret. He found it by the river, near where he saw that dead man in the water. That's so scary, Dad. Noah saw a dead man."

Jake snapped to full attention. "Tell me about Noah's secret, honey. What exactly did he find?" He tried to make his voice sound calm.

"It was just an old coin, like a big quarter or something. He had it wrapped up in plastic. But Noah said it might be worth more than a thousand dollars."

"And where did he say he found it?"

Kate shivered. "He said he found it along the river, right before he noticed that dead man in the water. Noah said it was a good thing Lightning was with him that day, or he'd have been too scared to move."

"Who's Lightning?"

"His dog, Daddy. You know. You've seen him around with his big yellow dog. Lightning's a nice, friendly dog. He doesn't scare me."

Jake's attention faded back out as Kate expressed her opinion at length on the pros and cons of dog ownership.

Could an old coin hold a clue to Shep's murder? He'd better send Dove to ask Noah more questions. The sooner the better.

Wednesday
October 31

"What's on tap for today, boss?" Deputy Dove pulled a metal folding chair next to Jake's desk and sat down, balancing a Styrofoam cup on his knee.

"Why don't you put that on my desk? The minute your restless leg starts jumping around, that coffee's on the floor." Jake moved a stack of papers, making a space for the steaming cup.

"Fair enough, boss." He set the cup on the flat surface and, as if on cue, his leg started shaking.

"Disaster averted. Now, here's what I'm thinking." Jake pulled out a legal pad and began to scan down his list. "What about Noah Lambert? I talked to him earlier, but the kid couldn't wait to get out the door and away from me. You help coach his soccer team, don't you? Maybe he'd open up to you. I have a strong feeling that boy knows more than he's telling us. And then there's the coin."

"Yeah. Of course, he doesn't know we know about the coin. Sounded like he wanted to keep it sort of secret. So I'll have to take it slow when I talk to him."

"We at least we need to take a look at it," said Jake. "I'm sure all

127

hope of finding any useful fingerprints on it is out of the question. He's probably showed it to all of his grubby-handed buddies. While you're there, I'm going make another visit up to Bessie Crawford's place. See if I can get anything more out of her."

"Good luck. She's a tough old bird, for sure." Dove downed the last of his coffee and tossed the empty cup into the trashcan. "I'll go talk to Noah. He's a good kid."

"Give Sissy a call on the way over. Just so she knows you're coming."

"Will do, boss."

Dove stepped out into the morning brightness. Although the sun was moving higher in the sky, the air still held a distinct autumn chill. He was glad he'd brought a jacket. He pulled out his mobile phone and keyed in the number Jake had written on the legal pad.

Sissy Lambert met him at the door.

"Good morning, ma'am." Dove touched his hat.

"Hey, Jason. It's nice to see you. Come on in. Noah should be back in a minute. He just ran a drink out to his papa. Harold's clearing out some brush in the back field. Want a cup of coffee? I just made a fresh pot. I also just made a pan of breakfast rolls."

The combined scents of cinnamon and coffee wafted from the kitchen, and although Dove had already eaten an ample breakfast and had drunk his caffeine quota, his mouth started to water.

"Smells wonderful, Mrs. Lambert."

"Come on into the kitchen and pull up a chair. I see Noah coming across the field now."

The rolls were soft, warm, and sticky. He pulled off a bite and closed his eyes in pure pleasure. He sure hoped he'd find a woman who could bake like this.

"Wipe your feet, young man," Sissy called out to her son as he approached the house.

Dove heard the back screen door slam and Noah came into the kitchen. "Hey coach. We gonna start weight training soon?"

"Hey Noah! We'll start in a couple of weeks. I just talked with the high school football coach, and he said that if we can schedule our training when his players aren't working out in the weight room, we'd be able to use their equipment."

"Man, that will be super cool. A real high school weight room? Wait til I tell Eddie and the boys."

Noah pulled a sticky roll from the pan and straddled the chair next to Dove. Sissy put a mug of milk in front of Noah, and sat down at the table.

"Should be a good deal, my man. But we have something else we need to talk about this morning."

Noah looked worried. "What do you mean, coach. Am I in trouble?"

"Not at all, buddy. Just the opposite. I think you might be able to help us solve a mystery."

"You're talking about that old coin I found, aren't you?"

Dove started to answer, but Noah interrupted. "Well, I've been thinking and thinking about it. At first, I was gonna keep it a secret. You know, maybe sell it and get rich. Surprise my mom and dad with a lot of money. But the more I thought about it, the more I figured I was being pretty selfish."

"How so?" Dove glanced at Sissy, and then gave Noah his full attention.

Noah pulled another roll from the pan and began to lick the icing off the top. He looked at his mother as if expecting a reprimand, but Sissy was intent on the conversation.

"Well, I found that coin the same morning I found Shep floating in the water. So I got to thinking. What if it fell out of his pocket when the bad guys threw him into the river? What if was a clue?"

"Good thinking, Noah." Dove pulled out a note pad. "Now, can you tell me where and when you found the coin?"

Noah looked at the notebook. "You gonna write it down?"

"Just make myself a few notes so I don't forget anything. That's okay, isn't it?"

Noah looked doubtful. "What if I get something wrong? Then it's in writing. I might get in trouble."

Dove patted his arm. "Noah, my man, I've known you since you were a wee boy. I've never in all these years heard you tell a falsehood. Not on purpose, anyway. I'm sure you'll tell me just what you remember."

Noah took a deep breath. "Okay. Well, like you already know, Lightning and me were going out to catch a couple of fish before breakfast. The grass was pretty wet, and it took us a little while to get comfortable. I was brushing away some of the dew so I could spread out my tarp. That's when I saw something shiny out of the corner of my eye." Noah took a gulp of milk. "I went down right next to the river and pushed back the plants and dirt. And then I found this silver coin, kind of between some rocks in the water."

"So you saw the coin before you found Shep's body?"

Noah nodded. "I was going to run home and look it up, but the library wasn't open yet, and I wanted to catch a couple of fish."

"And then, you saw Shep."

"At first, I thought I'd snagged an old shirt in the river," said Noah. "Then I saw his hand." The young boy shuddered. His mother moved closer to him and put her hand on his shoulder.

"That was pretty awful, I'm sure." Dove took a sip of his coffee and let the boy regain his composure. "Noah, I need to see that coin."

Noah shrugged. "Sure. Since I decided not to try to hide it, it's not a secret anymore. You can borrow it if you need to. But can I have it back when you're done?"

Dove smiled. "Probably. But it might belong to somebody else. Somebody who was robbed. I'll let you know what I find out, though."

"Okay, coach." Noah's voice reflected his disappointment. "I sure hope I can have it back, though. I really wanted to sell it. But I'll go get it for you."

Noah ran back through the hallway to his room.

"He's a good kid, Mrs. Lambert." Dove said. "You and Harold are doing something right."

Sissy sighed. "I worry about him, though. I worry about all kids growing up in this old world today. They have to see so many terrible things. You just can't shelter them anymore."

"Well, I don't know much about raising kids. In fact, my mama says I'm still a kid myself, but I think just giving him a good, secure place to come home to is one of the best things you can do."

Noah came back carrying a plastic bag. He handed it to Dove. "Take care of it, coach. We still don't know for sure what it's worth."

"I'll take personal responsibility for it, Noah."

"Oh yeah," Noah added as an afterthought. "I didn't let anybody touch it. I kept it in plastic wrap, like they do on T.V. The only fingerprints on it are mine and whoever dropped it in the river."

Dove whistled. "Good thinking, man. I'll have you on the force yet."

Noah gave his mother a sly look. "If that means I can quit school, I'll start today."

"Terri, you're a lifesaver," said Nanette, as she dropped her purse and a large bank envelope on a nearby table. "It's one thing for the three of us to have an idea to turn this house into a tea shop. It's another thing to make it happen. Good thing you came along when you did. I never could make head or tails out of spreadsheets. Emma uses them like they're God's gift to the business world, but not me. Give me a lead pencil and some graph paper any day."

"You're too kind," Terri murmured. She turned to Nanette. "We should be able to put things together in short order. You're lucky your friend left you all these vintage pieces."

She gestured toward the tables. "Those linens add an air of old world charm. And did you say you found china sets as well?"

"Oh yes." Nanette nodded. "Marguerite is working on counting them all today. She's out in the kitchen now. It used to scare me to death when Bertha served us tea in her mother's Royal Doulton. I always asked her for a mug instead. But she'd put a hand on her hip and say, 'Now Nanette, beautiful things are meant to be used, not stored away in a musty china cupboard.' The other day Jane found sets of Havilland and Bavaria as well."

"You're all set for tea service, then. Are you going to use that expensive china for guests, though?" Terri looked doubtful.

"Of course. I just told you what Bertha said about not storing things away." Nanette paused to straighten a fold in a drapery panel before she continued. "Now, Terri, you said we could get the business end of this operation running soon. Do you think we can open in December? Marguerite has her heart set on decorating the house for Christmas and having our open house right after Thanksgiving. You know, a sort of holiday kick-off?"

The ladies had reached the smaller parlor now, and Terri stopped to consider Nanette's question. "Yes, I believe we could be ready by then."

"Super. You know, at first I didn't think that we could even get this project off the ground. Now, I can't wait to get started."

Terri stopped in front of the bookshelf, eyeing a cardboard box sitting on top. She opened the lid and thumbed through one of the books inside. "*Custer's Mill – The Little Town with a Big Past*? What is this?"

"It's Lawrence George's new book. He owns the Bard's Nest in town. He asked if could put a display here. Custer's Mill is becoming a tourist attraction, and he thought the book would sell well here."

"He's paying you for the space, right?" Terri placed the book back in the box.

"Well…no. He's an arrogant sort, but he's still an old friend."

Terri looked at her in disbelief. "Your sentiment as a patroness is touching, but now that you, Aunt Jane, and Marguerite are business women, you have to think in a different way. Everything hinges on making money."

Before Nanette could reply, a persistent clanging of the doorbell interrupted the conversation. "Anybody home?" The door opened of its own accord, and

Alex George peered around it.

"Well, howdy to you. I was hoping you'd get here this morning." said Nanette.

"Nothing better than a warm welcome from one of the town's finest." Alex gave her a cursory hug and continued, "I brought the curio and thought maybe Marv or Petey Blue could help me get in the house."

Alex was not dressed for heavy labor. His khaki chinos and pin-striped Oxford shirt looked straight out of a New York fashion shop. As he moved into the hallway, the pungent scent of his aftershave trailed behind him.

"Well, the guys have left for the day. They're off to the library. Something about research. Maybe Hiram can help you. Hang on. I'll go see if I can find him."

Alex walked toward the parlor, almost colliding with Terri who was walking out.

"Oh. I'm sorry." They both spoke at once. Then they paused and said, "Excuse me" in unison.

Alex grinned. "We sound like a Greek chorus. Since we are already chanting in harmony, I suppose I should introduce myself? Alex George at your service." He bowed.

"Terri Allman. You might know my Aunt Jane."

"Seriously? You're Mrs. Allman's niece? She was one of the best science teachers I've ever had. Can't say that I was a remarkable student, though. Too many other interests at the time."

"Well, it looks like you've moved past that," said Terri.

"Looks can be deceiving, you know. But let's hope you're right." He grinned. "To what do we owe the pleasure of your presence, Miss Allman?"

"Terri. Please. My aunt and her friends asked me to do some work with them on their business plan. I might do a bit of financial recordkeeping for them as well. And you? What do you plan to put into this curio you're moving in?"

"Your aunt and her friends are letting my brother Laurence and me set up a sort of display in here."

"I see. So Custer's Mill is your hometown?"

Alex nodded. "My hometown, yes. My residence, no. I've just come back recently to help my brother regenerate the family business. An antique store. I'm afraid he's let the antiques part go, and concentrated on books instead." Alex shook his head. "Father would be devastated. He spent years traveling all over the place, collecting antiques for the shop. That's what I've been doing, and now I'm here to revive the business."

"Is that so?" Terri murmured. "Well, since you're a businessman, you'll understand that, in the best interest of my clients, we'll be charging you a monthly fee to rent the space."

"But…" Before Alex could finish his sentence, the door burst open and Nanette came in, Hiram in tow.

"Found him."

Hiram scowled. "I wasn't lost."

"Whatever." Nanette patted him on the back. "I'll leave you and Alex to your moving task. Terri and I will be in the kitchen if you need us."

Saturday

November 3

The shiny maroon Ford F-250 looked out of place next to Hiram's ancient green van.

"Nice wheels you got there, Mr. Steinbacher." Alex jerked a thumb in the direction of the van.

Hiram grunted.

"Still a man of few words, I see," said Alex.

"In the multitude of words there lacketh not sin." Hiram began to unhook the ratchet straps that held the curio fast to the truck bed.

"Now, if you raise the legs," said Alex. "I think I can maneuver this to the edge and then we can lift it down. Be very careful, though. It's an expensive piece." The padded cover gave no clue as to what was inside.

Gently, the two men lifted and lowered the cabinet to the ground. Each taking a side, they moved along the walkway, onto the porch and into the parlor. Only when the piece was settled inside, did Alex remove the heavy cover.

"There she be. Thanks man. Just help me slide it against the wall, and we're finished."

The curio was a perfect fit for the space. Alex stood back to survey it and gave a double thumbs-up. Hiram remained silent, his gaze fixed on the furniture.

"Like I said, we're finished," repeated Alex. "You can go back to your gardening, Mr. Steinbacher. Thanks again."

But Hiram didn't budge. "Where'd this come from?"

"Oh, around, I've been collecting unique pieces over the past five years." Alex ran his hand over the smooth wooden surface.

"Around." Hiram spat the word as though it had a bad taste. "Around? This looks like it belongs here. Right in Miss Bertha's parlor."

"Perhaps it does. But that's not where I got it. Anyway, I would never have guessed you would have an eye for antiques. Those other two pieces in the dining room are from the same period. 1850 English mahogany. Seeing that piece in the dining room is what inspired me to bring the curio as a display case for Lawrence's books and my jewelry. Beauty begets beauty."

Hiram gave Alex a level stare. "Do not store up for yourselves treasures on earth, where moths and vermin destroy, and where thieves break in and steal."

"Still quoting the good book, I see Hiram. Well, I don't think we have much to fear do we? That's one reason I decided to come home to quiet, little Custer's Mill." Alex paused, a slight smile playing on his lips. "No thieves around here."

Hiram stared at Alex for a full minute before he turned his back and walked away.

Alex shook his head. "Stranger and stranger," he muttered. He removed a microfiber cloth and a bottle of furniture polish from a case and began to rub the lemon scented oil into the wood. He sighed with pleasure as the wood grain began to shine even brighter.

"Gorgeous," he whispered as he unsnapped one of the black cases and lifted out several brooches. He placed them on the shelves, turning them so the stones caught the light. Next, he pulled out a necklace with three strands of pearls. A cluster of smaller pearls was inlaid in the gold clasp. "This beauty deserves center stage," he said to himself as he put the piece in middle of the glass shelf.

"Lookin' good, Alex." Alex was so preoccupied arranging his

merchandise that he hadn't heard Nanette and Terri enter the room.

"Very impressive," said Terri moving forward to get a better look. "My, these brooches are stunning. Antiques? They look expensive."

"Oh, no…nothing too exquisite. I buy at a lot of estate sales. You a jewelry appraiser too?" He said the phrase casually, but there was an edge to his voice that Terri did not fail to notice.

"No. But I know good pieces when I see them."

"Oh they're good pieces—good costume jewelry pieces, that is."

"Well, I don't think that pearl opera necklace is costume jewelry. Look at how each pearl is knotted into place."

"I suspect if you were to have it appraised it would be worth about thirty dollars."

Terri drew out her wallet. "Here's thirty bucks. I'll take it off your hands right now."

Alex drew back. "Not so fast, dear lady. I'm trying to build my display. Not take it apart."

"I should think you would want to make a sale when you can," said Terri, putting her wallet back into her purse.

"All in good time. All in good time. Just let me relish my dream for a few days."

Terri nodded. "Keep this up and you'll be out of business in a month."

"Hey. Come on Terri, we have to get down to the bank." Nanette scurried into the room, pointing at her watch. "It closes at noon."

"See you later, Alex. And if you change your mind about that necklace…" Terri started to follow Nanette and then turned back. "Don't forget what I said about the rent for the space. As their business partner, I'm only watching out for their best interests. You understand. It's just business."

The grandfather clock struck the quarter hour just as Marguerite nudged the kitchen door open, balancing a tray of china cups and saucers.

"Hiram, what are you doing in that corner?" The gardener was wedged next to the large buffet, in a precise location that afforded him a bird's eye view of the foyer and of Alex.

"Watching," said Hiram.

"Watching what? Alex? Us?"

"The eyes of the Lord are in every place, Keeping watch on the evil and the good." Hiram glanced over his shoulder and then walked past Marguerite and into the kitchen.

She heard the backdoor open and close.

"Goodness that man is a complete mystery. Now, we not only have a gardener, but we also have a watchdog." She set the tray down on a small table and looked around the parlor. "This old house has seen its share of good as well as evil. Let's hope the evil parts are behind us."

She gave a shiver and returned to the kitchen.

"I have to say I was a bit surprised you asked me to dinner in Mill City, Jake." Emma placed her napkin across her lap and looked around at the brightly decorated dining room. Indigo-colored grapes hung from sturdy vines draped around the room's parameter. Large posters advertising fine Italian wine covered the walls, and near the magnificent stone fireplace stood a life-sized statue of Dionysus, the Greek god of the grape harvest.

"I know Shep's case is taking a lot of your energy. I guess I thought all your free time was accounted for." She wiped the condensation from her glass of water and tried not to look at him.

"Well, I heard from a reliable source that you were eager to check out the food in this new restaurant," said Jake. "Besides, I wanted to get away from Custer's Mill for a change. It'll be nice to eat without an audience analyzing my menu choices."

The muscles around Emma's mouth tensed. "And we wouldn't want Miss Serafina seeing us together, now would we?"

Jake winced. This was not the way he'd hoped to start their conversation. "I just wanted a nice place where we could have dinner and talk. "Viva Italiano has been open only three months and already has rave reviews."

Emma leaned back in her chair and relaxed. "Well, I do love good Italian food. As you no doubt discovered from your reliable source. I suppose I could do justice to a fettuccine primavera."

Jake straightened the silverware so the edges were even. He was unsettled this evening, and from the sound of it, Emma was too.

He'd made a few misguided relationship moves lately. He wanted to clear the air with Emma. Being stuck on the mountain with Serafina had made him rethink the direction his life was heading. Why was he feeling so antsy? He had rehearsed his speech until he'd memorized it.

The waiter was dressed in black and white and sported a tiny bow tie. He bowed in Emma's direction and then turned his attention to Jake. "Welcome, my friends." He spoke with a slight Mediterranean accent. "Are you ready to order?"

"I am." Emma spoke before Jake could answer.

"Ah, a beautiful lady who thinks for herself. I like that." The waiter winked at Emma.

"I never trust my food choices to anybody else," she said. "I'll have the fettucine primavera, please. And the house salad."

Jake opted for the spaghetti and ordered a bottle of merlot.

Emma appeared almost at ease by the time the waiter returned with their salads. Jake closed his eyes. Now's the time, Preston, he told himself. He took a deep breath.

"Emma, I hope you're not getting the wrong idea about Serafina and me. We don't have anything going on. I mean, she knows the caves and I don't. I needed somebody to show me around. You know, going blindly into caves can be dangerous. And I needed to check out that area. Police business." Oh so smooth, man. Jake gave himself a mental kick.

"Sure. I get it. You got upset when I had a few ideas about Shep's death, but you're okay deputizing Serafina and making her part of the investigation. And giving her a black eye. Then you call your favorite babysitter when you're out and about with her. Good ol' Emma, she'll watch my kid for me."

Another dead end. Why was it so difficult to make women see reason? If she'd been a guy, they would have punched each other around a little and then all would have been forgiven and forgotten.

"Emma, you're a wonderful sleuth. You demonstrated that during the whole Brubaker murder investigation. You have great deductive skills."

"Oh yeah?" Emma leaned forward.

"Yeah. We made a good team last summer, but if you remember, you almost lost your life in the process. I don't want that to happen again."

Jake was aware he was turning red, but he kept going. "I have a selfish reason for wanting you to stay out of this Shep investigation. I care about you, Emma. I think I've known that for a while now. I have nightmares of you in that burning library."

Emma's face softened. "So you're worried that I'll be in danger if I become involved with this case? I appreciate your concern, but what are the odds of that happening again?"

Jake reached across the table and took Emma's hand. "Any odds are too many. And I admit it. I'm a worrywart. I worry about something happening to Kate. I still feel guilty for not going with my wife Mirabelle to the concert the night she died in the car accident. I could have saved her. I can't help it. I worry that everybody I love will be taken away from me. And I trust you with Kate. She loves you. We both…" His voice trailed off.

Emma squeezed his hand.

Jake was relieved to see the waiter approaching the table with a huge circular tray held above his head. So far, he hadn't stuck to his script very well.

"A fresh Italian feast for my guests." The waiter placed steaming plates in front of them and poured them each a glass of wine with a flourish. "Anything else I can get for you before I leave you to enjoy the fine food and fine company?"

They both shook their heads.

They were silent for a while, each struggling with pasta that insisted on sliding off their forks. Emma laughed and began cutting the slippery fettuccine into bite-sized pieces. Jake soon did the same with his spaghetti. "This might not be the Miss Manners way to eat long noodles," said Jake looking to see if the other restaurant guests were watching, "but it's the easiest."

"Indeed," Emma mumbled, her mouth full of pasta.

Jake reached across the table and brushed a crouton crumb from Emma's cheek. "Sorry if you were saving that for dessert."

"Are you kidding? I'm saving room for that chocolate-topped tiramisu."

"I like the way you think."

"Do you?" This time, Emma looked into his eyes.

Jake sighed. "Like I started to say, Emma, I've been doing some soul-searching. It hasn't been easy starting over again after Mirabelle's death. I brought Kate to Custer's Mill for a new beginning, and I think we've accomplished that. We've made new friends. Kate loves her school. She enjoys the attention she gets from Nanette and the other ladies at the library. And all those visits to Nanette's farm have opened Kate's world to wonderful new hobbies and ideas."

He paused. "Did you know? Last week she told me she is going to be a veterinarian when she grows up? She must have carted home every book the library has on raising and taking care of farm animals."

"Yes, I know all about how many books Kate checked out," said Emma. "Not a lot escapes my eagle eye. We even found a book on how to use insects as protein for farm animals."

"Oh lovely." Jake shook his head. "No girly-girl stuff for that gal. But back to what I was saying. Kate relies on you so much. I do too."

"Yeah, it would have been awkward for you the other evening when you and Serafina got stuck on the mountain if old reliable Emma hadn't been there to pick up your daughter."

"That's not fair, Emma. I know you care about what happens to Kate."

Emma sighed. "I know. I care about Kate. And against all better judgment, I care about what happens to you too."

Jake smiled. "I knew you'd understand."

"Whoa. Go back a minute. There's nothing to understand. I *am* reliable and predictable. Those traits that make you feel secure make me feel boring. In fact, your friend, Serafina, told me that I'm... What were her exact words? "Dull" and "stuck." And you know what? She's right. Except for college, I've never traveled anywhere. I'm living and working in the same town I grew up in. Now, how's that for exciting?"

Jake frowned. The conversation had gone off track again.

"What I'm trying to tell you, Jake, is that I need to climb out of this shell I've created for myself. Why, just the other day, Aunt Mia reminded me that we hold our choices in our own hands. We create our own destinies. I'm tired of waiting for Godot."

"Waiting for what?"

"Godot. The Samuel Beckett absurdist play. You know, the one where two guys spend a long time sitting on a bench waiting for someone who never appears. I can't remember if the guy they were waiting for even existed."

Jake still looked blank.

"Point is, there's no need for me to wait for a handsome prince to rescue me. I have everything I need right here." She gestured to her heart. "I'm ready for adventure, for roads that go ever on and on. Past Custer's Mill."

"At least I got the Tolkien reference, you'll be pleased to know." Jake forced a smile. "I hear what you're saying. I respect your Aunt Mia and her philosophy, but we both know that fate has a way of robbing us of dreams. I hadn't planned on being a single dad. I never thought Kate would be without a mom."

Emma's voice softened, "I'm sure you didn't. And I thought by now Eric would be a marine biologist and I would be a big city librarian. We'd be living in a geodesic dome somewhere on the west coast. Well, as you can see, my life is nothing like that."

"Nope. You're stuck in a small town on the east coast with a guy who is bumbling his way through dinner, tripping over his words and making a mess of things."

"Oh, it's not quite that bad, Jake, but it is time for me to move on. At least temporarily. I've settled things in my mind. Come spring I'm off to London, then to Paris and the Alps. That's one leg of the trip that Eric and I had planned."

Jake whistled. "Wow, Emma. When you decide to go, you go big."

"And who knows, maybe I'll find a job somewhere in my travels and decide to stay."

"Well, I for one hope not," Jake said ruefully. "But in the meantime, Emma, would you be willing to help us out with the investigation?"

Emma brightened. "What? You mean you want my input?"

"I don't want you gallivanting around all over Shenandoah Mountain, but I would like your insight on a couple of things. Like I said, you have an analytical mind." He grinned. He was about to add something about her emotions sometimes getting in the way, but thought better of it.

"Well sure." Emma looked down at her plate.

"Great. Why don't you stop by the station the next time you get a chance? And bring your notes."

"It's a deal, Jake. This will give me something to do while I wait for spring. I'm so glad I'm beginning to accept the fact that there is no outside control on my life. My choices are my choices."

"They are, indeed," Jake said. He wished he could say what his heart was feeling, but his words had spun themselves out. There was nothing left to say.

Monday

November 5

The first week in November brought with it even cooler temperatures. The folks of Custer's Mill were contemplating the size of their woodpiles, checking the amount of oil in their tanks, and cleaning out kerosene heaters. The wind had shifted to the northwest. Winter wasn't far behind.

The Chief's office was the warmest room in the police station. Jake had replaced the sleek, leather chairs and hard plastic sofa with wooden pieces covered in comfortable cotton upholstery. He exchanged rigid vertical blinds for accordion-style shades. And he swapped the harsh fluorescent lighting for softer track lights. The smell of freshly brewed coffee filled the air as Jake and his deputy discussed the latest developments in the Shep Crawford murder.

"Man, modern technology has come a long way." Jake handed Dove a copy of the forensics report on the tire treads from the mountain. "I was looking online the other day. There's a database of about 5,000 tire prints on record now."

"Will you look at this?" Jake whistled. "Looks like they found two distinct sets of tire prints near that cave. A 2010 to 2012 Ford

F-250 and an older model, smaller truck.

"Shouldn't be that hard to trace." Dove poured a generous helping of sugar into his black coffee and stirred. "Laurence George owns an F-250. And I know a couple guys just outside of town who drive them too. It's a popular truck with farmers."

Jake scratched his head. "Somehow, I can't see Laurence hightailing it up the mountain at midnight during a tree-ripping storm. But what about that smaller truck? Nanette? Or maybe those two mountain guys. I think Billy Brubaker drives a Dodge Dakota too."

"Nanette's about as likely to climb that mountain in her truck as Laurence is in his monster truck. It'd take a pretty good reason for anybody to make that trip under those conditions." Dove handed back the report.

"And yet," mused Jake, "somebody did. Two sets of people. Put in a call to the DMV, Dove. Check all of four-wheel drive F-250s registered in this area. I'll make a casual trip over to the Bard's Nest and see if I can catch Laurence. Even though I doubt that it's his truck we're looking for."

"Sounds like a plan, Chief," said Dove as he gulped down the remains of his coffee and reached for a stack of papers.

Jake parked the squad car in front of the Bard's Nest bookstore. He sat a moment to jot down some questions and think about the approach he'd take during the interview with Laurence. He'd start gently, but would bear down if Laurence was not cooperative. He could see the bookseller inside the shop now, talking with an elderly woman at the front counter.

The windows of the store were filled with antique bookshelves and tables displaying volumes of all kinds. A wardrobe with crackled white paint held children's books and a few stuffed animals.

It was a charming store. But Jake's task was not. He was there to find out where Laurence had driven his truck recently. And he intended to get a good look at the vehicle, too. Check the tread. See if there was mud on the tires or mud flaps.

The woman left the shop and stood a moment, wrapping her bright pink scarf around her neck. She gave Jake a curious glance before she hurried away down the street. Jake figured she'd go tell her friends the police were at the bookstore and what in the world could that be about. He shook his head. But that's unkind, he thought. True, maybe, but unkind to assume. "Time to focus, Preston." He spoke aloud. "Focus on the interview."

Jake had a gut feeling this could be the turning point of the investigation.

"Afternoon, Laurence," said Jake as he walked into the shop.

Laurence was dusting bookshelves. He glanced at Jake, and then carried on with his task.

"Hello, Chief, what can I do for you today? A nice hardcover copy of *Crime and Punishment* maybe?" Laurence chuckled at his own cleverness. He stepped away from Jake and started to straighten a stack of books on the front counter.

His body language was clear enough, thought Jake. He wants me to know this visit is an inconvenience and he has better things to do.

"Let me get right to the point, Laurence. The lab has analyzed tire tread from tracks at the likely scene of Shep Crawford's murder. Tracks I found a couple days after Shep's body was found. That tread matches the tires on your type of truck. So I'm interested in seeing your truck and talking to you about when and where you've been driving it. "

Laurence's face took on several hues of red. He bit his lip. He was giving his full attention to Jake now.

"What? That's impossible. I haven't…I didn't…" Laurence's voice trembled. He was frightened.

"Where were you the night of October 15th?"

"What? You can't think… What are you accusing me of? How dare you?"

"I'm not accusing you of anything. Right now, that is. But I need to know where you were and who can confirm it."

"I was at home, alone. So. No one can confirm it." Laurence's expression alternated between defiance and alarm.

His eyes narrowed as he struggled to regain his composure. Gradually, his mottled skin began to fade to normal.

"I see," said Jake. "I'd like to take look at your truck. Do I have your permission, or do you want me to get a warrant?"

"Be my guest." Laurence made a sweeping gesture with his arm toward the back door.

The truck sat parked close to the building in an alleyway filled with trash cans, cardboard boxes and recycling bins. The narrow passage led out to Main Street about four buildings down.

Jake stooped to examine the truck's tires. "Are these original?"

"Yes, it's a new truck." Laurence stood nearby, arms folded across his chest.

With a pocket knife, Jake dug out a sample of soil embedded in the tire and placed it in an evidence bag. It contained some of the strange blue-green soil he'd seen on the mountain. He took several photos of the tire tread. "I'd like to look inside," Jake said.

"Certainly." Laurence opened the driver's door until it touched the brick wall, but it was still a tight squeeze for Jake to climb in. He pulled on gloves and checked the seat and door compartments, then slid over to the other side. He swung the passenger door wide open in order to peer and grope under the seats. His efforts were rewarded with a small metal cylinder. A flashlight.

"Okay if I keep this for a while?"

"Of course. It's not mine, anyway." Laurence's haughty attitude had returned.

Jake placed the flashlight into an evidence bag. He'd have it checked for prints.

He was sure Shep's murder was connected to this truck somehow. He needed to confirm Laurence's whereabouts that night. He had more questions than answers.

"Laurence, I'd like you to stay out of your truck until forensics has a chance to check it over. I'll ask them to come today, so you don't have to go without it for long."

"Well, that's inconvenient. I need to pick up an order in Winchester." He paused; arms still crossed, and drummed his fingers on his sleeve. "I suppose it can't be helped. Far be it from me to stand in the way of truth, justice and the American way."

"Thanks. And they'll bring a warrant with them when they come. To make it official."

Jake paused at the door.

"And try to find someone who can confirm your whereabouts that night. Let's keep in touch."

When Emma stuck her head in the office door, Jake and Dove were deep in discussion about something on the computer screen. Dove was standing with his tall frame hunched over and his elbows propped on the desk, while Jake leaned forward in his office chair.

"Hi guys." Emma was happy. It was good to have her sleuthing hat on again, even if it felt a bit shaky. And she was especially happy because Jake had called again after their dinner date and asked her to come to the police station, saying only that he needed to talk to her.

"Hi, Emma, thanks for coming by. We'll be finished here in a couple of minutes. Have a seat." He pointed to a green chair next to the desk.

Emma sat, but she itched with curiosity. It took supreme effort to restrain herself from bombarding Jake with a raft of questions, and from going around the desk so she could see what they were looking at. But she sat in silence as the men completed whatever it was they were reviewing on the computer screen. Their faces were intent and serious.

At last, Dove stood. He placed a sheet of paper in the file basket on the desk and nodded to Emma as he left. She remained seated but craned her neck to get a glance at the paper. It was a list of people who owned Ford F-250s.

Jake was watching her. "Always looking for clues, eh, Emma?"

She chose to ignore the question. "So. What's up, Jake?"

"Looks like we've got a break in the case. I think your notebook might have something that will help even more. 'Course, I'll need you to keep our conversation confidential for now."

"Really?" Emma leaned back. "Of course, my lips are sealed. You can always count on that." She pulled out her notebook and began to flip through the pages.

"You know the other day, Emma, when you were going to tell me about the facts you'd collected in the case, and you mentioned a particular shade of soil?"

"Yes, right before you tried to silence me." Emma couldn't resist one dig. "Those painters. They were making a mess in the ladies' foyer. Jane noticed the soil tramped in from their boots looked unusual. The color, that is."

"That may turn out to be a very important clue, Emma. Do you think you can find any samples of that soil now? We want to see if it matches the sample I took near the cave where Shep was hiding out."

Emma blushed. "I just might have gathered a sample a while back. I just might have a plastic bag with a few teaspoons of the stuff in it."

"Well look at you. I think that deserves a promotion. Can you get that soil sample to me soon?"

"Sure. Not a problem."

Jake leaned back in his chair and linked his hands behind his head. "We're getting close now, Emma, I can feel it in my bones."

Jake stood and stretched. Emma allowed herself to watch him out of the corner of her eye. He must work out a lot, she thought.

"Emma, I know we talked this through, but I'm sorry I cut you short. Your powers of observation are a gift and I think you may have uncovered a key piece of evidence in this case."

Emma's heart soared. Not only was he a hunk, he was a grateful hunk. What could be better? She looked down at her notebook to hide her pleasure at his words.

"About your plans to travel. You working on those?" Jake pushed a pencil around his desk and kept his eyes from meeting Emma's.

"Oh yes. Every day after we close the library, I'm trying to work on my itinerary. This trip is going to take some careful planning to get everything in I want to see and do."

"That's great." Jake spoke without enthusiasm. "Sounds fun. Well, now I have to get ready to question those two fellas Dove's bringing in. Thanks again for coming by."

Emma rose to leave. "My pleasure, Jake. Call me anytime. Truly. And I'll bring that soil sample by."

Emma left the office, her heart light and her mind stirred to find even more details that everyone else had missed.

She had a gift.

"I know we're early," said Nanette, unwinding her bumpy wool scarf and setting a worn leather purse on the counter, "but Jane and I want to try to weed out the magazines before the crowd gathers. We have some *Better Homes and Gardens* that are at least two years old."

Emma sat at her desk, notebook open, and a travel brochure unfolded in front of her. She was so absorbed with her plans that she didn't notice that the library ladies had come in.

"Good grief child, have you lost your hearing?" said Nanette.

Emma jumped, and her pen fell to the floor.

"Are you okay?" Jane stooped to pick up the pen.

"Oh, I'm fine. I just lost track of the time. I'm so glad to see you. I've got a couple of things to talk to you about," said Emma.

"Well, I'll put on some hot water." Jane moved to the office behind the circulation desk. "I hope we can get in a cup of tea and a few minutes of chatter before the stampede begins." Jane set out three mugs and a box of Cinnamon Spice tea bags.

"Ladies, I have several important things to tell you. First, I made a major decision…a choice actually." Emma paused.

"Well? Are we going to know what that choice is?" Nanette said. "Jane and I aren't getting any younger. One of us could kick the bucket before you get this news out at the rate you are going."

"Oh, all right. Just ruin my dramatic moment," said Emma.

"You youngins and your drama." Nanette dropped a wrinkled paper bag on the floor and sat down at the small, round table in the library office.

Emma took a deep breath. "You know how Serafina has gotten under my skin more than usual lately? Like when she went on the mountain with Jake to show him those caves? And then she said those awful things about my being dull and stuck in a rut."

"Yes, dear, you did, and we all told you not to worry about what Serafina says or does," Jane said as poured boiling water into the mugs.

"Jane, let the girl go on or this will take all day." Nanette opened a white bakery box embossed with gold lettering and offered Emma a pastry. "Here. We stopped by Andes' Bakery this morning. That chef Craig is a marvel. He gave us a bunch of goodies to try out."

Emma chose an apricot scone. "Are you ready to hear my news?"

Nanette glared. "What do you think?"

"Okay, here goes. After talking with Aunt Mia and having a heart-to-heart conversation with Jake, I have decided to cross a big item off my bucket list. I'm traveling to Europe. I leave this spring."

"Well I'll say that's some news," said Nanette. "What do you think, Jane? Shall we let her go?"

"I don't think we have much to do with it. I believe her mind's made up," said Jane. "How long will you be gone dear?"

"Maybe a month. I have a lot of leave saved up. Isn't it exciting?" Emma poured a stream of sugar into her mug.

"You're going to go into a sugar coma if you don't stop putting that stuff into your tea." Nanette took the sugar bowl from Emma.

"Oops. Guess I wasn't paying attention." Emma poured more water into her cup to dilute the syrupy sweet taste. "But ladies, I'm going to travel to London, Paris, and the Alps. Just like Eric and I planned years ago. It was one of our dreams…an adventure. Aren't you happy for me?"

Nanette looked at Jane. "Well, it sounds like fun. Of course, we're happy for you. I think we're just a bit surprised that's all. You haven't talked about traveling or wanting to do anything more than be here in Custer's Mill."

"That's right, dear. We thought you were content with being a librarian, here among your books surrounded by friends who love you. More tea anyone?" Jane held the tea kettle aloft.

"I'm caffeinated enough, and I think Emma's full of sugar. We don't need any more." Nanette threw her tea bag into the garbage can and leaned toward Emma. "What will happen with the library while you are gone? A month is a long time to close the place, don't you think? We would love to help you out, but our tea room will be up and running…." Her voice trailed off.

"And maybe the bed and breakfast by spring," said Jane.

Nanette glared at her. "You're not only counting chickens before they hatch. You're counting eggs before they're laid."

"It's not out of the question." Jane set her cup down a bit louder than necessary.

"I guess I just need to get an assistant. There's so much to do around here. More than I can keep up with. Our library has become busier with all the new traffic through Custer's Mill. I think the town council will agree. We have the money in the budget."

The ladies exchanged glances again.

"Emma, you know we love you like you're our own daughter. We want the best for you. If you feel you need to go on this trip, then you should go. But, I hope it is for you and not because of something Serafina said or that you want to do this for Eric. You said you talked with Jake. Did you tell him about your trip?" Jane paused to wait for Emma's response.

"Yes, I did and that reminds me." Emma opened her notebook. "Jake and I had a long talk the other evening. He actually asked me for some advice about Shep's case. He said we should both move on and make some changes in our lives."

"Changes…what kind of changes? Child, did he say anything about how he feels about you?" Jane held her breath.

"Feels about me? Well, he told me I was dependable and that he was glad he could rely on me to help with Kate. And he did praise my analytical skills. He said I have great deductive reasoning abilities. As good as any trained investigator."

"Men…why can't they just say what they feel," said Nanette.

"Just remember, dear, you almost lost your life the last time you helped Jake investigate," said Jane.

"Jane, I love you dearly, but you worry 'way too much. Besides I don't know if I'll even be able to help at all."

"What do you know?" Nanette narrowed her eyes. "What are you hiding, Emma Grace Kramer?"

"Uh-oh. When you use all three of my names, I know it's serious."

"You'd better believe it. Murder is no laughing matter."

"Okay. So here's what I have so far. Noah found Shep in the river, but his body didn't have fluid in the lungs. So not drowned. He'd been hiding in the caves, but who brought him food? Was it Bessie? And there is unusual soil near the caves. The same green soil that I found tracked into the mansion.

"Yes," mused Jane, "I remember that soil. "

"My research indicates it has manganese in it."

"Wow, that's so interesting, Emma." Jane's eyes lit up. "It's rare, but not unheard of in this area."

"You know, Jane, I've been wanting to ask you where Marv and Petey Blue could have tramped around in such an unusual soil."

"You might find it in a few caves in the mountains," said Jane. "The valley floor is mostly heavy red clay."

"That would make sense. Those guys know the mountains like the backs of their hands. They also seem to be obsessed with some kind of tree. They're always 'researching' leaves and bark when they're in the library."

"They are quite an interesting pair," said Jane.

Emma fought back the urge to mention to the ladies that Jake thought there was a connection between the soil and the murder. And that she, Emma Kramer, had made that connection. But she was part of the case now. She couldn't give away too much information. She would keep her confidentiality promise to Jake.

"This place is full of 'interesting pairs' is it not?"

The ladies looked up, startled. No one had heard Serafina come into the library. "You'll be glad to know Emma, I used the door this time."

'Oh my." Jane looked at her watch. "We lost track of time. The library was to open five minutes ago."

Nanette looked at her watch. "We must have left the door unlocked when we came in a while ago."

"Relax, I'm the only one in so far. Now who are the interesting people you're talking about? And what do they have to do with caves and green soil?"

"Not that it's any of your concern, but we were just talking about some dirt Marv and Petey Blue had on their shoes last week. It made quite a mess in the foyer of the mansion which Jane had to clean up. That's all."

"I wouldn't clean up after those scoundrels. Jane, you're too good."

"Probably," said Jane. "But I'm much too old to change."

"Before we get any older," said Nanette, "we'd better work on those magazine discards."

"Fair enough. We'll check back in with you when we're finished, Emma."

"Sounds good. I have a lot to do this morning too." She pushed the power button on her computer and hoped Serafina would get the hint.

"Uh, Emma. Can we talk a sec?" Emma didn't answer, and Serafina continued, "I said some things I shouldn't have the other day. I'm sorry."

Emma didn't look up. All her attention seemed to be focused on the landscapes cycling through her screen saver. "That's okay. I've come to expect it from you, Serafina."

"Ouch. Are you going to play it cool? Like my words didn't hurt? I'm sorry Emma. I want you to know I was wrong. You're not stuck or boring or any of those things I said."

This time Emma looked at Serafina. "I know that. But in fact, I really need to thank you. It took your rudeness to help me see what was right in front of my nose. I have a great career and supportive family. And I still have time to accomplish those goals I had back in college. In fact, I'm planning a trip to Europe. The one Eric and I were going to take."

"Well, not any time soon I hope," said Serafina. "Jake needs your help solving this case. I need to talk to you about something that might be important."

"If it's about the case, I think you'd better talk to Jake."

"But you don't understand. This is serious. I overheard you talking about somebody having greenish dirt on their shoes. Well, some caves around here have dirt like that. We also found footprints and tracks near the cave entrance."

Emma opened the overdue book list on her computer and began to scan the columns. "I think Jake has everything under control. No worries. Now, I've got to get back to work."

Serafina sat on the edge of the desk and moved close to Emma. "I saw Alex at the warehouse around midnight, after we got back down the mountain. It was late, but I needed to check on the shop to see if the storm had damaged anything."

"Really? Ever think that Alex could have been doing the same thing? Checking on his stuff? What's so weird about that?"

"But he wasn't checking on storm damage. He was unloading something. Crates were everywhere. It just felt suspicious to me."

"Sounds normal to me. Maybe he just had a lot to uncrate. And why are you telling me this, Serafina?"

"Because you seem to have this uncanny ability to put clues together and come up with answers. I want you to find out what Alex is up to."

"So I'm supposed to tell Jake that Alex is up to no good because he was at his shop unloading crates late at night. Really, Serafina? Do you want Jake to think I'm nuts? No, second thought, don't answer that question."

"I'm serious, Emma. I have a pretty sensitive sixth sense. You know that. Something is not right."

Emma sighed. "Look, Serafina, I don't know what you're doing. I don't trust you. But if your extra sensory perception is giving you vibes, you go ahead and check them out. I, for one, am sticking to plain old, boring facts."

Wednesday

November 7

"Voilà, ladies." Chef Craig MacKenzie uncovered a silver tray and placed it on a linen covered table in the parlor of the Brubaker mansion. "Delectable pastries, all for your sampling and approval. Now close your eyes and pretend you're a guest at this tea room. You have taken your first sip of rich, bergamot infused Earl Grey tea. Now, you want to sink your teeth into a cloud of puffy sweetness that you'll remember for a lifetime."

The autumn sun shone through the front window, reflecting off the crystal vases, scattering a spectrum of colors across the room. Jane, Nanette, Marguerite, and Terri stared at the spread before them.

"What are we trying first?" Nanette scooted her chair closer to the table.

"Peanut butter truffles." Craig handed each woman a light brown, sugarcoated sphere.

"Food of the gods," sighed Terri. "Now if you could just find a way to take out the calories."

"Lovely lady," said a smooth baritone voice from the foyer, "calories are the last thing you need to worry about."

"Oh dear. Competition." Craig gestured toward Alex George as he entered the parlor. "Can't you let me have a chance at charming the ladies?"

"Nope." Alex leaned against the doorway frame. "All's fair in love and war. I'm afraid, my friend, you're on your own."

"I wish you'd stop talking about me as if I weren't in the room." Terri's smile took the edge off iciness in her voice.

"Sorry, ma'am. I didn't mean to offend. I'm not planning to stay long. I'm just unloading another set of jewelry out in front. There's a load of Louis VIII chairs scheduled to arrive at the shop in about quarter of an hour." Alex nodded to the group of ladies and disappeared as quickly as he had come.

Terri smiled to herself as she broke off a piece of poppy seed cake. Fascinating man. Enigmatic, but fascinating.

The ladies spent another half an hour tasting cinnamon vanilla teacakes, almond honey pound cake, and elegant French crepes. There was no doubt about it. Craig MacKenzie could bake. By the time he had wiped away the last crumb and packed his tray and serving plates into his case, the ladies were congratulating themselves on their luck. Craig's pastries would be a delightful addition to their tea shop.

"We'll make our final decisions and call you in the next week," said Marguerite, wiping powdered sugar from her chin.

Craig nodded and disappeared through the hallway.

"What a guy." Nanette looked wistful. "Wish I was twenty years younger."

"Twenty?" snorted Marguerite. "More like fifty."

"Don't quibble over a few decades." Nanette stood and brushed crumbs from her lap.

"Before you go," said Terri. "Can I talk to you all for just a minute?"

Nanette sat back down. "Why of course, child. What can we do for you?"

"I'm just curious about that jewelry Alex is selling in your shop. He seemed to think he was going to be able to take all of the profit without compensating you ladies at all for the space."

"We *are* just starting out," said Jane.

"No matter. You're giving him a superb venue. He needs to pay for the spot. And," Terri continued, lowering her voice," I can't help but wonder where he gets all of his stuff. Alex says it's not all that valuable, but he does have some nice pieces in there."

"He goes to a lot of estate sales," said Marguerite. "Probably finds the jewelry while he's shopping for bigger and better things. He has home furnishings in his antique shop, doesn't he?"

"I don't know," said Terri. "Maybe I'll stop by their store tomorrow after I finish at the courthouse. I'm picking up our business license, and a copy of the approval of the zoning permit. We need to keep on top of these things if we want to open in a few weeks."

She stood to signal the end of her part of the conversation. "It'll give me an excuse to keep an eye on Alex. I never trust a smooth talker." Terri winked at her companions.

Thursday

November 8

    Laurence George watched the early morning sun break through a line of thick, grey clouds. Unusual to see such a display in the east at this time of the year. In the summer, the dark, low hanging stratus clouds meant a heavy rainstorm. In winter, they signaled one of those rare nor'easters that occasionally ripped through the Shenandoah Valley, leaving record snowstorms in their wake.

    But eastern clouds in early November? He'd have to consult the almanac to see what weather they carried. That is if he could find the almanac. Every morning he noticed his book displays had been moved further and further back into the store. And every day, more and more books seemed to disappear completely.

    Laurence was sure his father would not approve of such an unequal division of the store space. In fact, the elder Mr. George always made it clear that he thought his boys should work together. Share the square footage.

    But their father, for all of his kindness and integrity, was naïve. How could he not see the path his youngest son was headed down? How could he have believed the smooth words for the lies they were? Laurence could only imagine the kinds of business dealings Alex had conducted in Europe. The haul of antiques didn't come cheap, and new deliveries seemed to arrive each day.

"Good morning, brother dear." Laurence cringed as Alex came through the back door of the shop, whistling bits of Yankee Doodle. "Trying to catch the worm, you early bird?"

"Trying to keep you from running me out of the store," Laurence said.

"Uh, oh. Touchy. I'm not taking out your stuff. I'm rearranging those dusty tomes. Not sure those old books give the best impression to our customers. I'm thinking a nice display of bone china pieces would attract a better crowd. I mean, Laurence, who in Custer's Mill reads Dickens anymore?"

"Charles Dickens was the greatest writer of all times." sputtered Laurence. "How dare you stoop so low as to criticize great literature? You and your ill-gained pieces of furniture couldn't even begin to match the aesthetic value of purely written prose."

Alex whistled. "Hold on, brother dear. We don't need you slipping into cardiac arrest or popping one of those bulging blood vessels in your temples. We'll leave the dear old Charlie D. where he is."

Laurence glowered. "Charlie D? Really? I don't appreciate your degrading sense of humor one bit. And another thing. Did you take my truck out the other night?"

"And why would you think that?" Alex became occupied with a dust spot on a nearby bookshelf.

"You heard me. My truck. Did you take it without permission?" Laurence's voice rose.

Alex scratched his head. "Let's see. Did I take your truck out? Well, I might have. I wasn't aware that I had to ask your permission every time I need it to get a load of furniture."

"I don't give a flying fig when you get your furniture. But I do care when you take my belongings without my permission. That truck is registered in my name and in my name only."

"Yes sir." Alex gave Laurence a mock salute. "Point taken."

"Is it now?" Laurence moved closer to his brother, and Alex could feel his breath on his cheek.

"And another thing. I want to know what you were doing on

North Mountain? With my truck? The last time I checked, there weren't any antique dealers in those caves."

Alex stepped back. "Whoa there. Wait just one minute. What do you think I could be doing on North Mountain? Like you said yourself. No dealers there."

"No? Then why did Jake Preston stop by to ask me about tire tracks he found on the mountain that match the tires on my truck?"

"Did he now? And that's a very good question. Why did those tracks match? Something you're not telling me, bro?"

"Don't 'bro' me." Laurence glared at his brother. "I don't know what's going on here, but I intend to find out. In the meantime, leave my books where they are. I don't want to see them moved one inch from their present location. Understand?"

Alex nodded. "Yes, I think I'm *beginning* to understand."

"And another thing," Laurence called out as Alex began to walk away, "leave my truck alone too. I don't want you moving it out of its spot. Not under any circumstances. I don't care if the place is on fire. You don't touch it. Are we clear?"

"Clear as a bell." Alex closed the door behind him.

Friday

November 9

"What's the address of this tea shop?" Nanette shifted the old truck into a lower gear as they entered Mill City. She'd been driving the Chevy Luv since 1979, but she still pushed the clutch in too late for it to glide in smoothly.

"It's a good thing I had my glasses frames tightened or you'd have jarred them right off my nose," said Jane. She gripped the door handle as the truck adjusted to its new speed. Let me see. I wrote it down."

"Here it is. 45 South Main. A Cuppa Fine Tea is next to the old pharmacy." Jane read from her notepad. "It should be easy to spot because of the green and white striped awning. Slow down, Nanette! I think I see it there on the right. Halfway down the street. Yes. There it is. Stop."

"Okay, okay. I see it. Don't jump out of your skin," said Nanette." I don't think the building will disappear while I look for a legal parking spot."

"I wouldn't want you to park illegally. You already have expired dates on your tags." Jane craned her neck to read the upcoming sign.

"Yes. There's a spot right in front of the door. This was meant to be."

Nanette pulled in front of the door and turned off the engine. She rolled up the mud-spattered window of the old truck, and tucked the keys into her pocket. "Maybe not getting a ticket for expired tags is also meant to be. Let's go in. I can see you're chomping at the bit."

"Well this is exciting. Who'd have thought last year at this time we'd be buying tea to serve in our own place?" Jane tugged at the rusty truck door as the hinges screeched in protest. "I used to have tea with Bertha here. This was one of her favorite places."

The tea shop was welcoming in a reserved sort of way. The myrtle green scroll sign announced the name of the place in penned Edwardian script. Painted lace curtains hung halfway down the bay window panes. A twisted iron ring knocker took up a large space in the center of the door.

"This place looks too rich for my blood," said Nanette. "Tell me again, why we needed to come here to Mill City to buy our tea? Serafina sells teas in her shop. Probably give us a good rate too."

"Really, Nanette. Sometimes I think if it were up to you, you'd just pull mint from your garden and stick it in a mason jar filled with boiling water." Jane smiled at her old friend. "Serafina sells herbal teas. We'll serve some of her teas. But this store sells only the best British teas. Bertha shopped here often. Like I said, I came with her several times. The owner is from England and has a wealth of knowledge about hosting a proper tea."

Jane led the way as the two friends stepped inside.

"May I help you?" A tall woman with a tweed skirt and cream-colored blouse came to greet them. "I'm Claire Davies, the owner of the shop." As she shook Jane's hand, her eyes widened in recognition. "Why, Jane, how nice to see you again. It's been a while."

"Yes, it has. This is my friend Nanette Steele." Jane pulled Nanette forward.

"I was so sorry to hear of Miss Brubaker's passing. Such a wonderful woman."

"Yes, we were all stunned." Not wanting to linger on their loss, Jane continued. "But, we've come to ask your help in finding out some information about teas. We'd also like to buy some supplies for our new tea shop."

She took a breath, not sure how much to share. "Bertha left her mansion to the two of us here and our friend Marguerite White. We want to honor her by opening a tea shop. She loved serving tea and her tea cakes were famous all over the county. We've already decorated the rooms with heirloom tables and buffets. We plan to use Bertha's English bone china. We'll also use the Royal Doulton she always used when she had us over to tea."

"Oh, I wouldn't use Miss Brubaker's family heirlooms. You risk them being broken. Besides, it's difficult to replace them these days you know. Those family heirlooms would make wonderful displays around the room though. And you won't have to worry about your patrons breaking them."

"We hadn't thought about that, had we, Nanette. Accidents do have a way of happening."

Nanette nodded. Several of Bertha's cups had perished at her own clumsy hands.

Claire continued. "You might consider using a newer version of the Blue Willow chinaware. You can replace them without too much expense. And you could serve the tea in various colored pots. Here, let me show you what I'm suggesting."

"The British prefer their Brown Betty's. It's the clay, you know, that enhances the flavor of the teas. We have several colors and sizes of tea pots. But I think you'd need the four cup size. You'll also need tea warmers or cozies as we call them. Let me show you those over here." Claire swept around the room pointing out the displays of tea pots, tea chests, cozies, and infusers.

"After we've finished selecting your tea accessories, we'll move to the tea tasting room and sample some of the various British teas you might want to offer to your patrons."

"This sounds like more time and money than we can spare," said Nanette.

Jane motioned for her friend to lower her voice. "Really, Nanette, It's the whole ambiance. The atmosphere of the place. This is what we need to give our customers a proper British tea experience. Bertha would expect nothing less of us."

Two hours later, Jane and Nanette emerged from A Cuppa Fine Tea laden with two large boxes containing a tea chest and several Brown Betty tea pots. An assortment of English, Irish, and Scottish teas and a variety of colorful tea cozies filled the two shopping bags. Nanette secured the boxes in the back of the truck, snapping the canvas cover in place. Jane put the bags behind their seats.

"I would say this was an expensive experience," Nanette slid into her seat and put the key in the ignition.

Jane nodded. "Perhaps, but, I think you also have to consider the valuable knowledge Claire shared with us about teas. We're new at this, remember. We need all the help we can get."

The truck sputtered and started with a jerk.

"The clutch, Nanette. Use the clutch."

"Hey, I've been driving this baby for more years than you can count on two hands. I know what to do. Don't go throwing me off track."

Nanette pulled out onto Main Street and headed west.

"Aren't you going to turn around? Can't we just go back the way we came?"

"There's a sign down here for Route 50. I think it might be a shortcut." Nanette took the next turn, following the signs.

Shortly after leaving Main Street, the buildings began to change. Plywood covered missing windows in abandoned houses. Lean, hungry dogs dug through tipped garbage bins.

"This place is starting to scare me, Nanette," said Jane. "Just turn around."

Before Nanette had a chance to answer, the truck gave a lurch and a sputter. The engine stopped cold. She twisted the steering wheel with both hands and drifted on to the wide shoulder beside the road.

"Well, that's just lovely." Jane unbuckled her seatbelt and turned around to look at the road behind them "Not a place I would have chosen to stop. That's for sure."

"Do you think I planned this?" Nanette got out of the truck and raised the hood. Steam poured from the radiator. "Overheated. I think if we give it a chance to cool off we might make it back to Custer's Mill."

"Then we'll turn around and go back the other way, right?"

Nanette glared. "Let's just get this taken care of first."

The silence was not a comfortable one. Jane pulled a brochure from her purse and read about the luscious pastries offered by A Cuppa Fine Teas. Neither woman noticed the large hooded figure that stepped out of the shadows and approached the truck from behind.

They both jumped when his face appeared in the window on the passenger's side. Jane gave a cry of distress. But Nanette laughed as she recognized the baker, Craig MacKenzie.

"Craig, you gave us old girls a fright. We didn't know you without your apron on."

"Sorry. I thought this was your truck, Ms. Steele. You ladies need a hand?"

"Please. The faster we can get out of here the better." Jane smiled.

Craig lowered his hood and glanced at the truck. "There's a good bit of steam coming out of your radiator. Think the water might be low?"

"Probably. It's been leaking a bit lately. I think I have a gallon or two of water on the back of the truck." Nanette offered him a muddy milk jug. Seeing his doubtful look, she said, "Don't worry, it's okay. The outside looks rough, but the inside is clean as a whistle."

"Super. Looks like the engine is cooling down now. Let me grab that rag back there. I'll put some more water into the reserve."

"Thank you so much." Jane gave a sigh of relief. "I didn't know what we were going to do."

"My pleasure," said Craig. He poured the water into the radiator, nodding at the satisfying gurgle. "There. That should do it, ladies." He tossed the empty jug on the back of the truck and gave a mock salute. "Start 'er up and see what happens."

Nanette turned the key, and after a few sputters and hisses, the engine turned over.

"Looks like you're good to go."

Nanette looked star struck. "Is there anything you can't do? First you overwhelm us with your baked goods, then you save our lives by fixing the truck."

"You flatter me." Craig smiled and flipped a stray dark curl from his forehead. "Safe travels for the rest of your journey. And make sure you get those hoses replaced as soon as you can. You don't want to be stranded again."

Nanette nodded and put the truck in reverse. "I think we'll turn around and go back the way we came. It's too late for a short cut."

"Shortcut, my eye," Jane said under her breath.

Jake felt a rush of excitement as he and Dove turned onto the steep roads leading into the national forest. This was the kind of police work he loved. The weather was perfect, and their hard work on the case was paying off. All they needed to do was find those two old mountain men and see what they were doing near the caves. Both Jake and Dove were almost certain that the second set of tire tracks belonged to Marv and Petey Blue.

"Keep your eyes peeled for any sign of the old truck those guys are driving." Jake's admonition was unnecessary. Dove tried to focus on every passing tree and hillside. The road became more and more rutted and they bumped along in silence.

"Stop, sir." Dove pointed into a thicket of rhododendron. "There is it, almost hidden, but not quite."

Jake pulled the Jeep as far over as he could, allowing the left wheels to rest in the ditch. Both men jumped out and wasted no time heading into the woods.

"You're a good tracker, Dove. You lead the way." Jake gestured into the forest.

"Over here, sir. I can see some broken sticks and disturbed leaves. Looks like someone was here today. Or at least since the last rain, day before yesterday."

Tramping through the thick underbrush was noisy. If Petey Blue and Marv were anywhere around here, they'd be sure to hear snapping and crackling before Jake and Dove could sneak up on them.

"Hold it." Dove held out his arm like a school patrolman, and cocked his head to one side. "Heard something." He paused, and the quiet of the woods surrounded them. A faint cry echoed from down in the ravine to the west.

They picked up their pace and walked as fast as they could. Branches and leaves slapped them in the face. As they came closer, they heard a man's voice shouting, "Marv. Marv, old boy. Where are you?"

Jake looked at Dove. "That's Petey, no doubt about it. And he's looking for his buddy. Let's let him know we're nearby."

Dove hallooed a greeting to Petey Blue. "Petey, this is the police. Where are you?"

Just then, they spotted the disheveled man through a stand of old-growth hemlocks. The forest floor was open underneath the grand old trees, and the men made quick progress. Petey stumbled and half-ran toward them.

"Chief Preston, Officer, I'm so glad to see you." He was breathing hard. "I can't find Marv. We were out here hunting for…er… hunting, um, mushrooms, and now he's gone. I've been calling and looking for him for the last hour and he don't answer. I'm scared. Please, you've gotta help me find him."

"Come on buddy. Settle down now. We'll find him." Jake's voice had a soothing effect on the distraught old man.

Petey sighed. "I'm so glad you're here. Last time we were together, we were over on the other side of that hollow there." He pointed through the trees to a steep, rocky bank running down to a stream.

"Well, come on, let's get over there and see if we can find him," said Jake. "Where were you two headed, anyhow? I don't believe you were hunting mushrooms. What were you doing out here?"

"We were hunting mushrooms." Petey's voice wavered. "Might as well tell you, Officer. We were trying to get back to one of those caves over there. We come across it a while back. It had a bunch of stuff in it. Expensive stuff. Old stuff. We called it our treasure cave."

"Oh? Were they *your* treasures?" Jake studied the old man.

Petey's voice was defensive. "We found it fair and square, and we wanted our just rewards. Nobody was there and we found it."

His face crumpled. "And now look what's happened. Marv's gone missing. No way would he shut me out of this. No way. Marv wouldn't do that, would he? Not to me."

He might, indeed, thought Jake. He might if he was guilty of murder.

Jake motioned to Dove to lead the way, and the three men picked their way down the rocks to the river. It was slow going.

Large boulders allowed them to cross over with only an occasional step into the fast-flowing water.

As they clambered up the bank on the other side, Petey called again, his voice cracking. "Marv! Marv! Where are you?"

No more than thirty minutes passed, but it seemed like an hour to Jake. They climbed over boulders and crunched through the leaves on the forest floor, calling out for the missing man.

Jake wondered how to break it to the old man that his friend might not be hurt at all. He might have flown the coop. Guilty of first-degree murder. And what was Petey doing the night Shep was killed? He'd have a long chat with the man when they were all back at the office.

Dove had moved ahead of Jake and Petey. His youth and athleticism were great assets out here in the forest. And he knew these hills.

"Sir, over here." Dove called out from behind a rock outcropping about 50 feet ahead.

The first thing Jake saw was an arm flopped over a large rounded stone. Marv lay face down on the ground. Dove leaned over him, feeling for a pulse. "He's alive, sir, but he's hurt." We need to radio for help.

"Yes, get back to the jeep and send an emergency call as fast as you can."

Petey Blue ran to his friend. "Marv? Marv? What happened, buddy? Don't you go dying on me now. You hang in there. You hear me?" He knelt down, tears streaming down his face. "Is he...dead? Do you think he fell? What happened to him?"

Jake shook his head, his face grim. "Looks to me like he was hit in the back of the head. He's hurt bad. But he's alive, and Dove's gone to call for emergency rescue. They'll be here soon. Maybe they can bring the helicopter as close as Fulks Run. Hope so."

Jake covered Marv with his jacket to help prevent further shock from setting in. The woods were almost silent as they waited for help, the stillness broken by Petey's sniffling.

A gust from a gentle breeze knocked a few acorns from a nearby tree and they fell into the dry leaves with a series of dull plops. In the distance two squirrels busied themselves burying fallen nuts for winter, oblivious to the human drama nearby.

At last the men heard sirens climbing up the mountain side followed by the whirl of a medical helicopter.

"Here they come, Petey." Jake put out his hand to help the old man to his feet. "They'll land Pegasus at the Ruritan Park and rush Marv down in the ambulance."

This turn of events was a new puzzle. Jake wondered why someone wanted to hurt Marv. Was Marv an accomplice? Or did he stumble onto something secret? This location was only about a quarter mile away from the cave where Shep had been hiding out. Was he part of the fencing operation? Or just in the wrong place at the wrong time? Jake hoped Marv could give him some answers, soon. If he pulled through, that is.

Saturday

November 10

The dust mop fell to the floor with a loud thunk. Jane sighed as she pushed the vacuum into the broom closet and bent to retrieve the mop. She shoved the door closed before anything else could fall out.

Someday, she'd find time to clean out that closet. But first, she needed to get her winter clothes out of Terri's room. The guest room, that is. Jane wondered how long her niece would be staying. She liked her guest rooms to be tidy, and Terri was not a tidy person.

Jane climbed the carpeted steps to the hallway leading to the bedrooms. When she opened the door to Terri's room, her shoulders sagged. The dresser was cluttered with cosmetics, and several pieces of wrinkled clothing were strewn around the floor.

Resolved to finish the job before her niece returned, Jane squared her shoulders and opened the closet. About three armfuls of winter clothes and coats were hanging there. If she moved them into her the other guest room, she'd be able to give Terri more space. Maybe Terri would actually put things away if she had more room.

Just as she was separating the first batch of hangers, Jane noticed a blue metal box on the nightstand. There was no lamp on the table.

The box took up much of the space on the narrow wooden stand and left little room for the half-filled glass of water perched precariously on the edge.

"I wonder what she's keeping in there." Jane spoke aloud. She felt disloyal, but admitted to herself a nagging doubt about Terri's innocence in her recent difficulties. She didn't want her niece to bring any dangerous baggage back to Custer's Mill. Especially not to the Brubaker mansion. Jane and her friends were working so hard on the tea shop. She just couldn't bear it if Terri did something to sabotage their business venture.

She opened the box.

Jewelry. Very expensive jewelry. She fingered a string of pearls and a gorgeous diamond ring. Were they real? Where had Terri acquired such fine pieces? A boyfriend? Or from a more nefarious source?

"Just what do you think you're doing, Aunt Jane?" Terri stood in the doorway, her face flushed with anger.

Jane jumped and dropped the box on the unmade bed. Her heart skipped a beat and she stammered an incoherent reply.

Terri strode across the room and grabbed the box. "You have no right to go through my things. What were you looking for? Pirate loot? I never thought you'd be so nosy, or I'd have stayed elsewhere."

Jane struggled to regain her composure. She was determined not to let Terri bully her. "Like where, my dear? Where? You're on the rebound from a near-miss indictment by your former employer, and you have no job. That's when we need family. And I'm sorry I snooped, but I just need to be sure."

"Sure about what?" Terri's eyes blazed. She tucked the box under her arm. "Sure I'm telling you the truth when I say Mrs. Jameson gave me—yes, *gave* me—some expensive items?" Terri paused for effect. "And some pieces I bought with my own money. Not that I need to answer to you about them."

"I just want to be sure things are on the up and up if you're going to work for the tea shop," said Jane, forcing her voice to keep an even tone. "The ladies are my friends, and you're my family. I feel trapped between a rock and hard place." Jane fought the tears that prickled her throat.

"Well, we need to come to an understanding, dear Aunt," said Terri. "While I'm here, I'd like to think this room is off-limits from snooping or prying. Think we can manage that?"

"Yes, Terri, of course. But I need to carry out the rest of my winter clothes from this closet. Then this room will be your private space for the rest of your stay. And speaking of that, any idea how long you plan to stay with me?"

"This incident makes me think I'd better be looking for other accommodations right away."

"Yes, I think that would be best. But please make yourself comfortable for as long as it takes for you to find another place."

Jane rushed past Terri and grabbed a double load of clothing from the closet. She fled from the room under the dark stare of her niece. She threw the clothes on her own bed and collapsed in a heap on the chair beside the window.

She was breathless and her heart ached for Terri. Had she mishandled the situation? Perhaps. But her mind raced toward a sad and unsavory conclusion.

Sunday

November 11

Petey Blue twisted the battered hat in his hands. Hospitals made him nervous. There wasn't a lot that got to him. He'd lived long enough to work through most of his anxieties. But he'd never get used to that smell. That terrible mix of medicine, disinfectant. Shoot, he'd just as well say it. Death. Hospitals smelled like death.

He watched his best friend as he lay still on the pristine sheets. Marv had never looked so peaceful. As long as Petey Blue had known him—and that had been since they were both boys—Marv had a sort of grungy look. His mama scrubbed his face until it chafed, but Marv still had the smudged look of a waif. Used to drive her crazy. "That boy attracts dirt like a magnet," she'd say.

But today, Marv was clean. His face pale, without a shadow. Pale and fading. That was the only way Petey Blue could think to explain it. Marv looked like he was fading away. The part that made him Marv was disappearing. Soon, he'd look like a shell. An empty cocoon.

"Heart rate and blood pressure looking good." The voice behind him startled Petey Blue out of his reverie. "Just not sure why his oxygen count is so low." A man dressed in a white uniform glanced at Petey Blue. "You a relative?"

"Best friend. Is he gonna make it, doc? What do ya think his chances are, doc?"

The young man looked amused. "I'm not a doctor. I'm the nurse on duty."

"A man nurse?" Petey Blue looked incredulous. "Now I've heard everything."

"You don't make it down from the hills much, do you, sir?" The nurse asked. "I can't offer an expert medical opinion, but most of his vitals are improving. Not sure what's with the oxygen level."

Monday

November 12

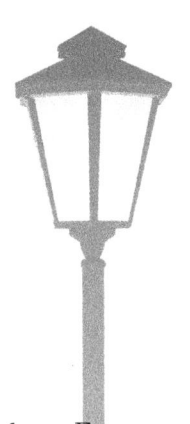

    A single red leaf floated past Emma as she closed the library door. This simple gift from nature made her smile. She couldn't imagine living in a place where seasons didn't change. It was nice to be out of the library and wonderful to breathe in the crisp autumn air.

    Thank heavens her volunteers had found time in their crazy schedule to take care of the library for a bit so she could take a break. Roast beef and gravy—the Spare Change Diner's lunch special for the day—sounded pretty tasty about now. Comfort food for a chilly day. She was about to cross the street when she heard someone call her name. Terri Allman waved to her from the other side of Main Street. "Going in here for lunch?" She pointed toward the diner.

    "That's where I'm headed. Care to join me?" Emma held her nose as Jacob Craun's tractor full of manure inched down the street. Small towns had their drawbacks, especially in spring and fall.

    "Nothing like fresh country air," said Terri, laughing. She held the door open and both women entered the busy din of the restaurant. Terri dumped a stack of envelopes on the nearest booth. "Okay to eat in a booth? I don't feel like hauling this load too much farther."

"Sure. What is all this?" Emma gestured to the paper pile.

"Oh, it's stuff for the tea shop. I've just come from the county registrar's office. I have the business license and the zoning permit. It's slow going, but we're finally getting everything in order."

"Those ladies are lucky you happened to come to town when you did." Emma pushed the menu aside and smiled as Kathleen, the waitress, stood, pen poised. "I'll have the roast beef special, please."

"Make that two," said Terri.

"Do you think they'll be ready to open in December?" Emma sipped her sweet, iced tea. The diner folks did sweet tea proud. Lots of sugar and strong orange pekoe. "That's less than a month away."

"You know, if you'd asked me two weeks ago, I'd have said 'no way,'" said Terri. "But the painting and remodeling are almost complete, and I think I can finish the paperwork by week's end."

"I must admit, I also had doubts about Petey Blue and Marv when I first saw them," said Emma. "But they've actually done a great job on the remodeling."

"I have to admit they didn't impress me that much at first either."

Conversation stopped for a moment as the waitress set down plates of roast beef and mashed potatoes smothered in thick, brown gravy. Although the menu still insisted the food dish was *purée de pommes de terre et sauce*, it was, in reality, pure southern fare. Meat and potatoes.

"Looks delectable." Terri unfolded her napkin and pushed her hair back. "By the way, Emma, if you have a second after lunch, want to go to the Bard's Nest with me? I promised Alex I'd stop by and see some of his antiques. And today's as good a day as any."

"Antiques, eh?" Emma winked.

"Of course. What did you think?"

"Oh, nothing. It's just that Alex has a kind of charm you don't see much in Custer's Mill."

"Really, Emma? What about that new police chief? Jake, I believe he's called."

"Touché." Emma smiled. "If we're going to the Bard's Nest, let's skip dessert here and have scones at Laurence's cafe in the back of the store. Their scones come from that new bakery, and they're fantastic. The coffee's not bad either."

* * *

If Emma hadn't been so familiar with the buildings in Custer's Mill, she would have hardly recognized the Bard's Nest. In just a few days, it seemed to have gone from a bookstore to an antique shop. They opened the door to a maze of furniture, tables, chairs, and chests of all sizes and shapes.

"Yoohoo. Anybody home?" Emma called.

"Be with you in a sec," came a voice from the back room. "I need to find a place to put this plate before I drop it." Alex came through the curtain carrying a thin, ancient looking piece of china. "Why, look who's here!"

"Told you I'd stop by." Terri pretended to study the intricate carvings on a cedar chest. "Emma and I had lunch at the diner, and she said save room for scones here."

"One of the best moves my brother managed to pull off. Buying scones from the Andes bakery and grinding his own coffee beans." Alex set the plate down on the counter and dusted his hands on his khaki pants. "Speaking of business moves, how's the tea shop coming along?"

"Not bad. Picked up the last of the legal work today." Terri was still studying the cedar chest.

Alex chuckled. "They did a good job when those ladies hired such a hard-nosed business woman—a person of action."

"And you're not? A person of action?" Terri smiled.

"Looks to me like you've acted quite a bit," said Emma, surveying the crowded shop. "I'd be hard pressed to find any books at all in this so-called bookstore."

"Who said it was a bookstore? Our father didn't start this business as a bookstore. That was the work of my dear brother. It's a good thing I came back before Laurence destroyed everything Father had built up. The antique business would still be history without my timely intervention."

Alex looked at the two women. His expression changed from annoyance to charm in mere seconds. "Well, follow me, ladies, and I'll serve you both with the cafe's best—iced blueberry scones and pure Colombian coffee."

The dessert and coffee lived up to their mutual reputations. Both women vowed it wouldn't be the last time they ate at the Bard's Nest. Emma glanced at her cell phone. Lunchtime was long over. She sighed. Mondays. She had to get back to the library.

"Well, Terri, this has been so relaxing, but I'm completely stuffed and I need to get back. I'll slip into the restroom before I leave. You can head out if you want. I don't see Alex around." She held out a five dollar bill. "Here's my money. Can you pay him? He can keep the change. Or are you in a hurry too?"

"No hurry." Terri smiled. "And it's my treat." Terri waved away Emma's money.

"That's very nice of you, Terri," said Emma. "You'll have to let me return the favor soon. Bye now."

Terri found Alex in front of a cherry curio cabinet arranging jewelry on the lighted shelves. She handed him the check and a twenty dollar bill. "Keep the change. That dessert was outstanding."

"Many thanks. That's quite a tip! See anything here you're interested in?" Alex gestured to the entire shop.

"Nice collection you have here, Alex," Terri said. "Is most of this stuff from your European travels?"

"Not so much. I made a lot of contacts in Europe, but it's so darn expensive to ship things back and forth."

"I'm surprised you came back to a one-horse town after living the good life overseas." Terri picked up a turquoise necklace and ran it through her fingers.

"All I can say is that's a good thing I did. A year or two more, and everything Father worked for would have turned to ashes. My brother has no clue how to run a business."

Alex turned to Terri. "And you? Why are you here? The pace of living can't compare with what you must have been used to in D.C."

"How'd you know where I came from?"

"Seriously? Don't you know how small towns work? A pretty girl comes to town and every single guy within shouting distance is updated on her personal history." Alex smiled and Terri turned her attention back to the necklace.

"Really? That fast, huh? Would you really like to start tongues wagging? How about having dinner with me soon? Just as friends," she added.

"Sure. I'd love to. I'd be crazy to turn down an offer from such a fascinating lady." Alex tapped the calendar on his phone. "How about tomorrow evening? I'm free then. Or is that too short of a notice?"

"It's not like my calendar is brimming, Alex. Tomorrow evening is fine. I'll call you."

As if on cue, Alex's cell phone gave three shrill rings. "Sorry, I've gotta take this. I'll be right back."

"Not a problem," said Terri. She watched Alex walk through the doorway. He forgot to lock the cabinet and she didn't bother to remind him. The sound of his steps became fainter as he moved into the small room at the back of the shop. She looked around to make sure no one else was near. She didn't want an audience.

Silently, she lifted the glass top and picked up an expensive ladies' watch. This was not costume jewelry. Turning it over, Terri recognized the jewelers stamp. Just as she thought. She had taken this exact watch to be repaired for Mrs. Jameson.

"So how did you get here?" Terri spoke softly as she turned the watch over to caress the smooth back.

"Who are you talking to?" Emma's voice made Terri whirl around like a guilty child.

"Emma. I didn't hear you come back into the shop." She replaced the watch and closed the lid. "I was just admiring the jewelry. Alex had to take a phone call."

"Well, I've got to get back. Are you going to wait for Alex?"

"No, I'm ready to leave. I've paid the check. And I think I've seen all I needed to see."

Alex's face was dark as he watched the women from his post just inside the back room. He made no move to see them out.

The library was quiet when Emma returned from lunch. Jane sat at the front desk and Marguerite shelved books in the children's section. Emma had enjoyed her break. It was good to know that even though she'd been gone a bit longer than expected, the library was still running smoothly. She was lucky to have such dependable volunteers.

"Thanks, Jane. Looks like everything is ship-shape. Has it been this quiet the whole time I've been gone?" Emma eased into her chair and tapped a key to refresh her computer screen.

"Pretty much." Jane smiled. "Did you have a good break?"

"I did, and you'll never guess who I had lunch with?"

"Hmmm. Let's see. Does he wear a uniform? Is he new in town and rather handsome?" Jane kept her eyes on the screen as she scanned another book.

Emma pulled out a file folder from the side drawer and started to thumb through the papers inside. "Good guess, but not this time. I met your niece, Terri, on my way to lunch. She joined me at the diner. We had the roast beef special."

"Oh, that's great. Terri needs some friends. I worry she doesn't have anyone her age to talk to," said Jane.

"We had dessert at the Bard's Nest after lunch at the diner. She and Alex both seem to know a lot about antiques." Emma pulled the top sheet out of the file and started to type the information into her computer.

"I must confess that is a side of Terri I don't know much about," said Jane. "I do know that she came in contact with some pretty well-off people when she worked in Northern Virginia. Her employers, the Jamesons, had a beautiful estate and a lot of exquisite furniture. Many of the pieces had been family heirlooms, I gather."

"She didn't mention anything about her past job," said Emma. "We mostly talked about the tea shop. I'd like to get together with her again. There aren't many people my age in Custer's Mill either."

"I sometimes think she misses the fast-paced life in Northern Virginia. I know she used to call and talk about the fancy parties and social events she attended with the Jamesons. Terri has such an imagination. Why, she'd describe—in great detail, I might add—the guests, the food, and even the jewelry the women wore. She always tried to estimate what these soirees cost. She seemed to be able to put a price on almost everything."

"I'm impressed." Emma said. "I must be her polar opposite. I'm horrible at numbers. And I wouldn't know a diamond from a rhinestone. But that would explain her interest in the estate jewelry Alex was putting out on display."

"Jewelry? I thought he dealt in furniture. Except for the few pieces of costume jewelry he put in the tea shop," she added.

"He has a bit of everything in that store. China, cedar chests, estate furniture, and a pretty impressive collection of jewelry."

"What does Laurence think of this sudden shift of merchandise?" Jane asked.

"Not sure. I haven't talked to him for a while. I can't imagine he's too happy with his books being moved farther and farther back into the recesses of the store."

Jane shook her head. "There's bound to be a civil war between those two before this all ends."

Emma nodded. "By the way, Terri seemed to take a particular interest in a piece of jewelry. A gold watch.

Jane laughed, "I don't believe anyone in our family would be able to afford a gold watch. And believe me, if I did, I wouldn't sell it."

A gust of wind lifted the paper Emma had placed on top of the file and set it flying into the air. Emma looked up to see Serafina standing in the doorway

"Will you please close that door, Serafina? We don't have the money in our budget to heat Main Street. Besides, what are you doing here in the middle of the day? Don't you have a shop to tend?" Emma was annoyed that Serafina could still make her hackles rise.

"I've had a rash of customers and couldn't get away until now." Serafina stopped to catch her breath.

Jane placed the pile of books she had just scanned onto a cart. "It's time for Marguerite and me to get back to the mansion. Terri is bringing us the final registration papers today."

"You don't have to leave, Jane." Emma glanced at Serafina. "This won't take long."

"No, really. I need to get back before Nanette sends out a posse to find me." She nodded toward Serafina. "Enjoy the rest of your day."

Jane walked toward the back of the library. When she was out of earshot, Emma turned to Serafina. "So, now that you've scared my help away, what do you want?"

If Serafina noticed the aggravation in Emma's voice, she chose to ignore it. "I wish you would take this whole Alex thing I told you about seriously."

"You're telling me to be serious? That's a laugh. You, the free spirit telling me, the old soul, to be serious? And what 'thing' are you talking about?"

Serafina moved closer to Emma and lowered her voice. "This isn't funny. Something bad's going on here, and I'm afraid somebody's going to get hurt."

Serafina continued. "I had asked you to see if you could figure out what Alex is really doing at the warehouse. Remember we talked a few days ago? So what's the deal? Did you find out anything?"

Emma was getting impatient with her insistent visitor. "Why are you seeing demons behind every bush? You're always making fun of me for playing Jane Marple. Why have we switched roles?"

Serafina was silent for a long time. When she finally spoke, her voice was hesitant.

"Do you remember when I was a kid, and I could sometimes tell when something bad was going to happen? That wreck on I-81 that killed Rita Dove's nephew? The derecho storm that came through and wiped out the trailer park outside of town? The fire in the old downtown theatre?"

"Speaking of fire, you weren't too clairvoyant the night Eric was killed."

"Emma, listen to me, please. I know I don't do things the way you do. I don't live life the way you choose to live it. We have different ideas. But I need you to hear me. There's something bad happening at the warehouse. Call it my intuition, my telepathy, or whatever you wish. I have a strong sense of foreboding. Please take me seriously."

Emma had never seen Serafina so disturbed. "Okay. What's worrying you?" She turned from her computer screen and gave Serafina her full attention.

Serafina took a deep breath. "Last night I heard Alex talking to somebody. It sounded like they were discussing their inventory, and how they needed to 'hurry up and get in touch with the fence.' That's a middleman for thieves."

"You don't have to explain street talk to me, Serafina. And why are you telling me? I'd think you would welcome the excuse to tell Jake all of this stuff."

Serafina sighed. "Would you let it go? For one minute could you think of somebody other than yourself? I'm serious. I believe something is brewing, and it's not pretty. You know Jake won't listen to me. I don't have any solid evidence and that's always what the cops want. I just have a very bad feeling about all of this."

Emma turned back to her computer. "Okay. I'll mention your suspicions to Jake, at least. He might want to come by and ask you some questions. Will you be around this evening?"

"I'll be at the diner. I'm filling in for Kathleen at five."

"I'll see what I can do." Emma looked up, but Serafina was already gone.

Alex left the shop and walked down Main Street. His mind raced. He turned at the alley that led to the town park, crossed the humpbacked bridge, and eased down on a well-worn bench facing the river.

That girl was too smart. He wasn't sure why she had asked him to dinner. Other women might have fallen for his charm, but he could tell by her shrewd look that she knew there was something suspicious about his business dealings.

He pulled out his phone and tapped a message. 'Meet me at ten tonight, usual place. Urgent.'

He pressed "send" and tucked the phone back in his pocket.

Some middle schoolers walked by and stared at him. He stared back, his mind far away, thinking, planning. Somehow, he had to get out of this mess. But how?

Alex stayed at the Bard's Nest late into the evening. He'd told Laurence he had a lot of paperwork to take care of. That was true, but his paperwork was stored in a safe at the warehouse.

Earlier in the evening, he'd eaten a sandwich at the Spare Change Diner. It seemed like hours ago now and his stomach growled.

He hated waiting. But he had to sit tight until the sun went down. It would be better to slip out into the dark night. After most residents were settled in their homes.

A sleepy town like Custer's Mill rolled up the streets by 7 p.m. He'd waited until 9:50. It was time.

He locked the front door of the store, and moved down the street toward the warehouse. A muted glow came from the Herb Shop, but there was no movement inside. He pushed on the side door to his room. Someone had already unlocked it.

"Did anyone see you?"

"No, I was careful, but what difference would it make if someone did? It's our warehouse. Everyone knows I keep antiques here. Deliveries come all the time." Alex's voice was unsteady. "It would be more of a problem if someone saw you."

"Yeah, I guess. But nobody would think I'd be doing something like this. They have no idea. What about that shop in the front? I saw a light."

"I glanced in the window as I came by. No one was there. It's just a night light. Serafina's shop closes at five. She works evenings at the diner. No reason why she'd be in her shop now." Alex said.

"So, what about this cryptic message you sent—what's urgent?"

"I'm not sure." Alex knew he needed to choose his words carefully. His partner had a tendency to act first and ask questions later. "Terri Allman has been real curious about our antique business lately. She just moved here from the Washington D.C. area. She might know something about that rash of break-ins. I found through my dear brother's gossip network that she was accused of embezzling from her former employer. But she got off the hook and they didn't end up pressing charges. I don't know. Maybe I'm just gun shy. I'm having dinner with her tomorrow evening, so I hope to find out more."

"Well, you'd better find out fast. We don't need anyone snooping around now. Not when we're so close to the final deal. It's taken us a while to put this operation together. Our buyers are ready. We have the deliveries set up. Everything's gone by the book so far. Except for that run-in with the two country bumpkins on the mountain."

"Yes, and you almost killed that man. In fact, we still don't know if he's going to make it. Was that necessary?" asked Alex.

"I'm not letting anyone get in my way—that includes this woman. You understand what I'm saying?"

The two men stood in the shadows as they talked. Their voices carried throughout the cavernous space. Their conversation drifted into Serendipity's packing area. Serafina crouched against the wall, not daring to breathe. She'd heard everything.

Tuesday

November 13

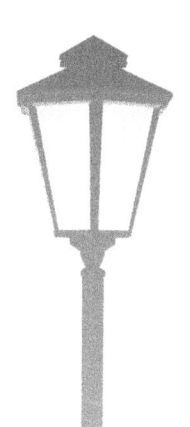

Petey Blue didn't put a lot of stock in praying. From what he'd learned in Sunday school, God's will was always done. So it didn't make much sense to ask for something. If God wanted you to have it you would. If he didn't, all the asking in the world wouldn't do any good.

A girl he knew once told him about St. Giles. The old Greek guy lived in 600 A.D. and was the patron saint of hermits, beggars, and poor people. Maybe he'd understand Petey's plight. Maybe he should pray to him.

Marv was all he had left in the world. Sure, there was Bessie, but she didn't seem to care if he lived or died. In fact, most of the time he thought she was plotting ways to poison him. Maybe use that same tea concoction that killed old Bertha Brubaker.

Why had he insisted that they try to get some of Shep's civil war treasures from the cave? Those old pieces meant nothing to him, now that his friend was dying. Why, even those thirteen young saplings behind Bessie's house were worthless without Marv to help him watch them grow. He remembered Hiram saying something once about not laying up treasures on earth. Well, he'd give everything he owned right now, on the spot, if Marv would just recover.

He started as the double doors in the waiting room swung open, and a man in a white coat approached him. Petey steeled himself for the worst.

"Mr. Crawford?" Petey Blue rose and looked up at the doctor, trying to read his face.

"Marv. Is he…?"

The doctor smiled. "Please, sit back down." He motioned to the blue vinyl chair. "I have some hopeful news for you. Against all odds, it seems your friend may pull through. But he has a rough road ahead."

Petey Blue was glad he was sitting. The great wave of relief that washed over him came in the form of extreme dizziness. He didn't hear much more of what the doctor said. He didn't need to.

Marv was going to be all right. That was all that registered. That was all he needed to know.

"This is the oddest diner I've ever seen," Terri slid across the seat and put her purse beside her. "When Emma and I ate here yesterday, she told me the guy who started this place wanted a French bistro. Imagine that. A French bistro in this one-horse town."

"Hey, don't make fun. You've got to admit it's a colorful story."

"Yeah, sure. Hey, I see cafe au lait on the menu. Is it the real stuff?"

"The real stuff minus vanilla beans, cinnamon and cocoa powder," Alex grinned.

"In other words, plain black coffee with a shot of heavy cream?"

"You got it." Alex passed a menu across the table. "What do you fancy, my dear?"

"I may need a translation. My French is not up to par."

They settled on *Filet de Porc Sauce Normande*.

Terri leaned back in her seat and surveyed the room. "Quaint. I wouldn't say it looks French. I guess the blue-checked table cloths do add a Provençal touch. By the way, is that a grocery store out front?"

"Yup. Everything from diapers to pipe wrenches. There's also a whole rack of Pinot Noir. Wanna take a bottle with us on our warehouse tour tonight?"

"I'd recommend the Riesling." They looked up to see Serafina Wimsey at the end of the booth, iced tea pitcher in hand.

Both Alex and Terri froze, forks in midair. "Well, well, well. If it isn't the herb girl." Alex said. "Will your talents never end?"

"Jack of all trades. That's me. From the sound of scraping crates, I'd say you're pretty busy at the warehouse. You must be doing a lot of 'trading' of a different sort."

Alex glanced at Terri. "Lots of crates coming in now. I've gotta stop buying soon, and start selling. Right, businesswoman?"

Terri rolled her eyes. "You do like to stereotype, don't you? I would hope that simple rules of economics—you know, supply and demand—would answer that question for you."

"You should watch him," Serafina jerked a thumb toward Alex. "He's a slippery one. He has all of the right pick-up lines, but he's not real careful who he uses them on."

"I'm pretty sure I can take care of myself." Terri broke her roll into bits and made a pile along the side of her plate.

"By the way, Serafina," said Alex, "I'm giving Terri a tour of said warehouse after dinner this evening. So if you hear noises, it will only be us."

Serafina set down the tea pitcher and looked at Terri. "All jokes aside, be careful. Crazy things can happen when we least expect them."

"Say what?" Terri looked amused. "I grew up in the D.C. metro area. I would imagine I'm a bit more street savvy than the average Custer's Mill citizen. I believe I can take care of myself."

"Just be careful, okay?" said Serafina. She turned and disappeared into the kitchen.

"Well. You must have convinced her that you're a big bad wolf, Alex dear." Terri placed her hand on his arm. "No worries on my part. I'm a pretty sophisticated Red Riding Hood."

Alex covered her hand with his own and smiled. "I think we both know our way around the woods."

"But I am curious," said Terri pulling her hand away. "Just what did she mean about the activity at the warehouse? I thought you sold your wares at the Bard's Nest."

Alex sighed. "Do I come across as a total cad? Seriously?" He spoke as if explaining a complex idea to a young child. "I do sell my 'wares' at the Bard's Nest. Right now, the warehouse is a drop off spot. I have my orders shipped there. Eventually, I want to branch off and open my own shop in the warehouse. But for now, it's a place where I store stuff. Make sense?"

"Perfect sense." Terri smiled. "Now, let's change the subject."

"Most gladly. You said you grew up in the D.C. area. Where did you live before coming to the metropolis of Custer's Mill?"

"Falls Church. I worked for the Jameson estate. Ever heard of the Jameson family?"

Alex rubbed his chin. "Can't say as I have. Are they famous or something?"

"Famous against their will, I would imagine. Their faces were splashed all over the metro news when their mansion was robbed."

"Oh yeah? They must have had some valuable stuff to get that kind of publicity." Alex shifted in his chair and glanced out the window. A full moon was just beginning to peek around a curtain of clouds, creating an eerie glow on the almost bare trees.

"They did. A lot of heirloom stuff. Their ancestors migrated from Poland. Apparently they were wealthy in the old country too." Terri followed his gaze out the window. "Perfect night for a witches ride."

"Got your broomstick oiled?"

"I suppose there are a couple of ways I could take that statement, so I'll just ignore it. But back to the Jamesons, a lot of the stuff that was stolen is irreplaceable. You know, not only valuable but sentimental."

"Were they targeted?"

"Come on, Alex. I know you live in Custer's Mill, but you can't tell me you haven't heard about the string of break-ins and robberies all down the east coast."

"Well, yeah." admitted Alex. "I believe I remember reading something about it in the Post."

"I would have thought you'd be interested since part of your inventory seems to be heirloom jewelry."

Alex sighed. "I wish my stuff was as valuable as you seem to think it is."

"Alex," said Terri. "I know some of your things are valuable. Why do you insist on trying to convince me otherwise?"

"You know," said Alex, "if you're so blasted curious about my stuff, let's get out of here and go over to the warehouse now." He grabbed the check and walked toward the counter.

"Well, well, well," Terri murmured, following behind him, "looks like I've stirred the inner beast."

The answering machine blinked as Emma entered her townhouse. She'd had so many spam calls lately that she didn't even bother to listen to the three messages her machine held for her. She switched on the kitchen light and opened a can of Fancy Vittles for Molasses.

Today hadn't been horrible. In fact, much of it had been quite pleasant. She wasn't sure why she was so tired. She had some more notes to make before she forgot the details of the day.

Emma still hadn't said anything to Jake about Serafina's strange conversation at the library. Maybe Serafina did have a sixth sense. But how did you explain that to a rational policeman? Jake's world dealt in facts. Not premonitions.

A sharp rap on the door startled her. "The Raven," she muttered. Who but Poe's black bird of woe would be bothering her on the only evening of the week she could relax?

Of course. It was Serafina. Her long, ginger hair flew in all directions, her skirt was twisted, and beads of sweat stood out on her forehead.

"Get your coat, Emma. We have to go to the warehouse. Now."

"Serafina, get hold of yourself. What's going on? What happened?"

"Please, Emma. We don't have time for this. You have to come with me. Terri's life is in danger."

"Terri? What does she have to do with anything? Serafina, you're acting like a wild woman. If you insist that I go with you, at least let me drive. I don't think you're capable of handling a vehicle at the moment." Emma pulled her coat from a hook by the door and followed Serafina to the car.

"It's like old times," muttered Emma. "Serafina leading and me following."

Serafina slid her key into the door of the herb shop and motioned for Emma to follow. The small, blue globe behind the counter gave the women enough light to make their way to the back of her shop. They walked in silence through the hallway between the Serendipity Herb Shop and Alex's room in the back of warehouse. The door was open a crack, and they heard male and female voices.

Crouching low, both Emma and Serafina had a cramped view of the room. Three people stood next to a stack of crates. They could see Terri and Alex. Another man faced away from the doorway.

"I knew you were up to something." Terri's voice shook, but her resolve increased as she spoke. "You didn't fool me. Did you forget? I'm a shrewd businesswoman. And, by the way, your display in the Bard's Nest wasn't such a good idea. I recognized a gold watch. A piece of jewelry that once belonged to my former employer. A piece of jewelry that had been stolen."

Serafina's sudden painful grip on Emma's shoulder almost made her cry out. Emma balanced herself against the wall and pried Serafina's hand away.

"Calm down," Emma whispered to her companion. They both needed to keep their wits about them. Panic would make them do something stupid.

"Come on now, Terri." Alex's voice had dropped to a whine. "You can't blame me for everything. I'm just a regular guy trying to make a living. You can't imagine that Althea Jameson missed one piece of jewelry. That family could buy out the entire town of Custer's Mill."

"I hardly think your crimes are limited to petty larceny," said Terri. Her words were no longer shaky. So far, the other man had not made a sound.

Emma pulled Serafina away from the door. "Do you have your phone?" She mouthed the words and pantomimed a holding a phone. She didn't want overreact, but she was sure she saw a gun in the stranger's pocket.

Serafina nodded.

"Good. Go back outside and call 911," whispered Emma. "Tell the dispatcher we need Jake at the warehouse right away. Hurry. Tell them it's a crime in progress."

Serafina nodded and crept to the front door. For the first time in their checkered history, Emma realized she was in control of the situation. But there was no time to gloat. She turned her attention back to the sounds from the other room. The voices had gotten louder. Peeking through the opening of the doorway, she could see the stranger. Now the gun wasn't in his back pocket. It was in his hand. And he was pointing it at Terri.

"Well, well," the stranger said. "It's a pity we have to end our relationship before it even started. You, my dear girl, might be a savvy businesswoman, but you are not very wise in the ways of really big business." He moved a step closer to her, the gun still pointed at her chest. "You could have come to me privately if you had concerns. Why, we might have even been able to make a deal."

"I would never make a deal with a thief." Terri spat out the words. "I'm not a thief."

"Hmm. Others have thought differently. Like the Jamesons. *They* think you're a thief. You hurt my feelings, Terri. But it doesn't matter. I won't hold a grudge against a dead person. And you, my dear lady, are going to die."

"No." Alex pushed past Terri and stood in front of her. "No more killing. Violence was not part of the deal. I'm out. It's over. Take your stuff and leave. I won't say anything, and I'm sure Terri won't either."

The stranger gave a soft laugh. "Really now. Is that how it works in your fairy tale world? I say 'sorry', take my loot and leave, and you forget you ever saw me? Even if I did believe you—which I don't, by the way, it's much too complicated for such a simple solution. Now step away from the lady, Alex. I'll deal with you later."

"I won't. I've had enough. I'd rather die than be part of this operation." He moved closer to Terri, covering her with his body.

A shot rang out. Someone screamed.

Emma ran into the room just as Alex crumbled to the floor.

Jake propped his feet on the coffee table and leaned back on the sofa. It was ten-fifteen, and he had tucked Kate into bed hours ago. He'd finished the dishes and the laundry and settled down to catch up on the stack of magazines that seemed to grow taller by the day. He probably should cancel some of the subscriptions. At least until he retired.

His phone beeped. Never a good thing at this hour. It was dispatch. An urgent call to a crime in progress at the old warehouse. He grabbed his gun.

Just as Jake slid into the driver's seat of his car, Dove pulled up, spraying gravel as he skidded to a stop. Good, thought Jake. Dispatch had also notified Dove as requested. By previous agreement, whenever Jake was needed on an urgent off-duty call, Dove would stay with Kate until one of her sitters could arrive. Then he'd follow Jake to the scene. Small town police forces had to make do with small staffs.

Jake sped toward the warehouse, approaching it from Myrtle Street. He decided to avoid using his siren. If there was a crime in progress, he hoped Emma wasn't around. Her sleuthing abilities were outstanding, but she'd already been through one life-threatening event. His heart beat hard as he switched off the flashing lights and swung his patrol car onto the paved drive behind the warehouse. He could see a truck beside the loading dock.

Lights shone in the back of the old building, and a dim lamp lit Serafina's tea shop. He walked cautiously through the shop into the hallway, his back to the wall.

He pulled out his gun and held it in his right hand. He crept slowly along the hall.

Someone was crying. A woman.

"He shouldn't have tried to save you. What a fool he was." The angry male voice was muted in the back room.

"And what about me? Are you going to kill me too?" The woman's voice quavered.

Jake felt a split second of relief. That wasn't Emma's voice. He edged closer to the door.

"I suppose you killed Shep too? You kill anyone who finds out about your side business?"

Jake froze. *That* was Emma's voice. No, not again. Jake knuckles turned white as he gripped his gun with all his strength. He forced himself to take deep breaths and stay calm.

"It's not a side business, missy. It's big business. Rob from the rich, sell to the rich. Make a good living that way." He chuckled. "And that's right. I keep things clean. Don't like worrying about loose cannons. Like you two. You stuck your noses in my business and now you'll have to join your friend Alex."

His voice became tense. "Now get out that door and into the truck. We'll finish this business elsewhere. Then I'll be back for his body. Leave no trace. That's my motto."

Jake heard the unbalanced bravado in the man's voice. He would have to focus all his skills to get to the man before he took off with the women. And before he'd use the weapon that'd already mortally wounded Alex.

Just then the side door of the warehouse opened, letting in a tiny stream of light from the street. Jason Dove's face peered around the door frame. Jake could see his hand. His gun was drawn.

Jake motioned to Dove to join him. Thank God. Now they could take the man. At least he hoped they could. "Go around back and come in by the loading dock," Jake whispered. "Quick. He's about to kidnap Emma and another woman. I think he's already killed a man, so be careful. This is a bad one."

Dove disappeared. Jake readied himself to kick the door wide open. He heard feet shuffling and quiet crying. They were leaving the building. Now was the time to make his move. Now or never. He drew in a deep breath.

The door cracked open with a loud thud, and Craig MacKenzie turned his Magnum 45 on Jake as he pushed through the doorway.

"You." MacKenzie's face twisted into a sneer.

"Shoot me and you go down, too, MacKenzie." The two men stood, guns and eyes leveled at each other for a long, silent minute.

The silence was broken when MacKenzie's arm jerked backward, and his gun fell to the ground with a crash. Dove had him in a chokehold. He kicked the gun away.

Jake ran to Alex who was lying on the floor. He felt for a pulse. It was faint, but it was still there. He was bleeding heavily. "Emma, do you have your phone?"

Emma nodded, numb.

"Call an ambulance, quick. Alex is still alive. Barely." Jake saw an old drop cloth lying on the floor. He spread it over Alex, leaving only his face exposed.

Jake turned to MacKenzie, who watched him with a chilling, malevolent gaze.

"Nice work, Dove. Cuff him, read him his rights, and call for another car."

"Craig MacKenzie, you're under arrest for the murder of Shep Crawford, and the attempted murder of Alex George."

Dove's voice faded away as Jake walked around the stacks of boxes to where Emma and Terri stood. Emma's arm was around Terri's shoulders as she continued to weep.

"It's okay now, Terri." Emma's voice was soothing. "Craig's been caught, and Alex is still alive." Emma's eyes met Jake's and she raised her eyebrows. Both knew there was a slim chance Alex would pull through with the amount of blood he'd lost.

"Emma." Jake couldn't find any other words to say. He fought to keep his voice from cracking.

Keeping one arm around Terri, Emma took Jake's hand and squeezed it. Sometimes, words were unnecessary.

As the sound of sirens got closer, Dove led Craig MacKenzie out to the street for his ride to jail. Emma, Terri and Jake followed. Jake knew there would be interviews to conduct and reports to complete. But right now, he drew comfort and relief from just being in Emma's company. Kate was right. Emma made him happy.

Epilogue

Saturday, December 1

The grandfather clock chimed the quarter hour. Three-fifteen. In forty-five minutes, the Compass Rose Tea Room would open to the public. But right now, the spacious parlor was empty. The evergreen garland that lay across the fireplace mantel swayed in the breeze generated by the vintage Georgian ceiling fan. It infused the room with the fresh smell of the forest. Tiny white lights twinkled around archways and windows. Music box holiday carols chimed in the background. Miniature Christmas trees were centered on each table, and delicate lace ribbons graced the backs of the chairs.

If anyone had come into the tea room at that moment, they would not have seen the elderly lady standing by the frosty window. They would not have noticed her soft blue eyes or her wistful smile. She looked out over the parlor as if trying to take in every detail. The starched white linen tablecloths, the Royal Doulton china with the hand-painted holly leaves, the sparkling silver spoons, and sprigs of cedar tucked into brass napkin rings.

This was not the time for her to indulge in memories, but she couldn't help but recall past Christmases in this parlor. The elevnen-foot tree that grazed the surface of the plasterwork ceilings, the wrapped packages, the sound of sleigh bells as her brother and father hitched up the wagon to Molly, their old mare, to carry the family to midnight services.

She had left too soon, to be sure. But not much too soon. Her spirit was more restful now, her vision more clear. God was in heaven, and all was right with the world.

"Nanette, you can't let Petey Blue into the tea room in that grungy denim jacket." Marguerite balanced a plate of petit fours in one hand and a Brown Betty teapot in another. She jerked her head in the direction of the foyer.

"Oh relax, Marguerite. Everybody knows Petey. They wouldn't expect him to be dressed in tails and a bowtie." But Marguerite had already moved on. Nanette shook her head. There was no way she'd disturb her old friend, Petey Blue. He was so disappointed that his buddy, Marv was not able to come to the opening. But the fact that Marv was still alive was a miracle. Anything else was just icing on the cake.

Jane Allman saw Laurence George standing alone in one corner, and she walked over to greet him. She was surprised but glad he decided to come tonight. His brother, Alex, had died from his gunshot wound just before Thanksgiving. Jane knew from experience that the happy Christmas season was especially poignant for people who were grieving. Her heart went out to him. But Alex's brave stand had saved Terri's life. To Jane and her friends, Alex George was a true hero.

Kate Preston and Noah Lambert collected coats at the door and hauled them to the spacious bedrooms on the second floor of the mansion. Noah had been disappointed to learn that the coin he found in the river was one of the heirlooms stolen from the Jamesons. But a two-hundred-dollar reward from the family softened the blow. And now he'd decided he wanted to be a policeman instead of a forest ranger when he grew up. He was hoping for a crime-solver kit for Christmas.

Jason Dove and his aunt Reba were filling cups with hot cider for the guests to sip as they waited. So far, most of Custer's Mill had turned out to witness the grand opening of the Compass Rose Tea Room. The young man looked longingly at the platters piled high with holiday treats. They were waiting on Hoyt Miller to arrive to cut the ribbon.

"Can you believe this place?" Emma looked around in wonder. The ladies had shut everyone but themselves out of the tea room for the past two weeks while they fine-tuned the decor. "It's gorgeous."

"Incredible," said Jake. "I knew they'd do an amazing job, but I had no idea it would turn out this impressive."

"They've kept the spirit of the place." Emma's great-uncle, Albert, and her Aunt Mia joined them at the bay window.

"Wouldn't it be just perfect if it would snow?" Emma sipped her cider and watched as the clouds gathered, gray and billowing. The bare branches of the old maple trees swayed to a tune only they could hear.

"He's here." Petey Blue's voice was as excited as a child's. "Hoyt's here."

The old black Lincoln pulled up outside the door, and two men stepped out. Emma squinted to see who the other man was. Billy Brubaker. Of course. Billy should be here. He had deep ties to the place his family used to own.

The crowd parted and made way for Hoyt to walk to the foyer door. He carried an enormous pair of scissors designed for the occasion.

"Before I cut the ribbon and start the celebration, I want to first thank each of you for coming out on this cold December afternoon. I know you're busy with decorating, baking, shopping, and all of the other chores that come with the holiday season. But it means a lot to me, and I'm sure it means even more to the industrious ladies who have taken on this enormous project and have seen it through so beautifully. We're family here in Custer's Mill. Oh, we have our spats and differences, but what family doesn't? We've been through a lot recently, and have lost some of our own. But today, we need to focus on our gains, not our losses."

"Hear, hear," someone shouted.

In the back of the room Hiram Steinbacher wiped a tear from his eye. He hoped no one noticed the chink in his steel armor.

"And now, I'm pleased to present the Compass Rose Tea Room." Hoyt snipped the ribbon and a loud cheer erupted.

"Sit where you wish," said Jane over the rumble of the crowd moving toward the parlor and the delectable foods waiting to be consumed.

"That was useless," said Nanette. "You know very well people are going to sit anywhere they please. This is Custer's Mill."

The quiet observer couldn't resist one last peek at the celebration—her friends all arranged around the room in boisterous groups. The hand-painted holiday Royal Doulton, she suspected, would weather a few cracks and perhaps even complete shatterings. Nanette would be handling it, after all. But she always believed in using the beautiful dishes every day, and she was glad her friends were using it today.

But it was time for her to go back to her gentle resting place, and that was fine. She blew a kiss into the room.

Outside on the stoop, Serafina sat alone, looking out over the almost barren garden. Life was fragile and there were no guarantees. She'd made so many mistakes. Seen so many losses. Her mother. Eric. Bertha. Shep. And now Alex.

The old lady touched the girl's shoulder as she moved on down the lane. She disappeared behind the hedge of rosebushes.

Serafina's heart lifted. She was not aware that the ethereal touch had given her courage. Courage to acknowledge that there is goodness in the world. She smiled as a few snowflakes landed on her cheeks.

It was time to get back to the party inside.

About the Author

Mary Fulk Larson is

- Mary M. Smith, Ed.D., who enjoyed a thirty-year career as a public school teacher, university professor, and curriculum developer, and now offers her services to community and church organizations;

- Tammy Fulk Cullers, M.A. Ed., who teaches middle school English, grows low-maintenance plants, plays piano and collects green glass; and

- Barbara Larson Finnegan, M.B.A., master gardener, neophyte farmer and small business owner.

Cumulatively, the authors have ten grown children and ten grandchildren, and live with their husbands in the lovely Shenandoah Valley.